"Oh, we'll find them homes, right enough," said Dad, easily. "I'll ask around at work, you ask around in school."

"Yes, you might make some new friends that way," said Mum. "You can invite them over to see the kittens."

As their parents went on discussing the problem of finding homes for the kittens, James sat silently scowling at the honey pot and Jenny looked deep into her cup. So far neither of them had even mentioned the kittens to anyone at school; they had no intention of inviting anyone to "choose one for themselves".

As far as James and Jenny were concerned, the six kittens belonged to Breakfast – and to them.

HIPPO ANIMAL

Take Six Kittens

Bette Paul

Scholastic Children's Books,
Commonwealth House,
1-19 New Oxford Street,
London WC1A 1NU, UK
A division of Scholastic Ltd
London ~ New York ~ Toronto ~ Sydney ~ Auckland

First published in the UK by Scholastic Ltd, 1998

ISBN 0 590 19895 5

Typeset by
Cambrian Typesetters, Frimley, Camberley, Surrey
Printed by
Caledonian International Book Manufacturing, Glasgow

10 9 8 7 6 5 4 3 2 1

Chapter 1

"Hurry up and eat your breakfast, James," Mum said, passing quickly through the kitchen. "The school bus will be here in ten minutes."

James pushed his cornflakes about until he could see the spotted Dalmatian at the bottom of his bowl. He looked at the dog's head, dreamily. Maybe that was just the kind of dog they'd get, now they'd moved out of town.

Both Mum and Dad had agreed they should have a pet now they lived in the country. James's sister, Jenny, wanted a pony, though they both knew she'd never get one. James thought he'd have a better chance of

1

getting a puppy – a little puppy, who would only need a basket to live in, and a garden to run in, not the stable and field a pony would need.

Dogs are easier than horses, he thought, tipping his bowl towards him so that he could see his Dalmatian.

"Hurry up and finish your breakfast, James." Dad was stacking the dishes into the dishwasher. "I want to load this up before we go."

James sighed. He hated being rushed in the mornings. Slowly, he scooped up a spoonful of cereal and caught another glimpse of the dog at the bottom of the bowl.

"You said we could have a pet when we moved out of town," he reminded his dad.

"We will," Dad promised. "Just as soon as we're settled."

"Will we have a Dalmatian?"

"We will not," said Dad. "Dalmatians need lots of exercise and somebody around them all day." He went over to the door. "And if you don't get a move on in the mornings, we won't get a pet at all," he warned.

James took another spoonful of cereal and sighed.

"Haven't you finished yet?" Jenny dashed round the kitchen, collecting school things. "I'm not waiting around all day for you – we've got to catch the school bus, you know."

"I *know*," said James.

Mornings never used to be like this, he thought. When they lived in town, school was only just round the corner, Mum's office was a ten-minute walk away, Dad's workshop a short drive in his van. Nobody had to leave before eight-thirty so mornings were very easy and relaxed.

But now they lived in the country, in a beautiful new house made out of an old stone barn. Soon Mum would have her office up in the roof-space and Dad would set up a craft workshop in the outhouse at the back, so they could both work from home. Meantime, they had to drive back into town to work while James and Jenny caught the early school bus. Everybody was in a terrible rush in the mornings – except for James.

3

"Hurry up, James, *please!*" called Mum from the bathroom. "Finish your breakfast and come and clean your teeth."

James picked up his 101 Dalmatians mug and took a sip of milk. And as he sipped, he heard a small squeaking noise. He looked at the picture on the mug.

"Was that you?" he asked the Dalmatian.

But the dog didn't answer.

Instead, another squeaking sound came from the open door. James lifted his head from the mug, looked across the kitchen and saw the source of the small, squeaky sound: a little cat stood peering round the kitchen, as if she knew the place! James sat quite still and watched the cat.

Ginger, she was, with a white bib, a tiny pink nose and huge golden eyes. When she saw James she stepped across the tiles and rubbed herself against the table leg.

"Miaow!" she said, in her little squeaky voice. And she opened her little pink mouth wide.

"Are you hungry?" James asked. He tipped the rest of his cornflakes into Jenny's empty yoghurt-and-fruit carton and poured the milk from his mug on top of them.

"Do cats eat cornflakes?" he asked her.

This one did. She quickly lapped up all the cornflakes and the milk and then ran across the kitchen and out of the door. James picked up the yoghurt carton and dropped it in the waste bin.

"Finished at last?" Mum said when she saw James's empty bowl and mug. "Great – you've just got time to do your teeth."

So James went off to the bathroom, smiling to himself. But he didn't tell anyone about the cat.

* * *

Every morning that week, the little cat came into the kitchen just as James was finishing his breakfast all on his own.

On Tuesday, James gave the cat a blob of scrambled egg on Dad's yoghurt lid.

"Hurry up and eat it before we have to go," he told her.

On Wednesday, he poured some of his porridge on to Mum's plant-pot saucer.

"Hurry up and eat it before she sees you," he whispered.

On Thursday, he put bits of buttered toast down on the doorstep for her.

"Hurry up and take it away," he said. "We're off now."

On Friday, the little cat was enjoying the remains of James's boiled egg so much that he had to chase her out when he heard Dad coming downstairs.

"You're getting quicker, James," said Dad when he saw the empty eggshell. "You've finished your breakfast on time every day this week."

"He doesn't seem to hurry though," said Jenny. And she looked at him suspiciously.

James pulled a face at her and dashed off upstairs to collect his school bag. Glancing out of the bedroom window, he saw that the little ginger cat was curled up under the old drystone wall which divided their garden from the fields below.

So she hasn't gone back home, thought James. I wonder where she lives?

Saturday was the best day of the week. Nobody got up early, nobody started rushing around, nobody cared whether James ate his breakfast quickly or slowly – or even whether he came down for breakfast at all. But this Saturday James made sure he came down early, just in case the ginger cat was around. Dad was already in the kitchen, making a pot of tea.

"Fetch the milk in, James, please," said Dad. "I'm taking a tray up to Mum this morning."

As James opened the kitchen door to pick up the milk, the little ginger cat slid between his legs and stepped daintily across the floor as if she owned the place.

"Miaouuuuuw!" she said, rubbing her back against Dad's legs.

"What's this?" asked Dad, peering down.

"A cat," said James.

"Of course it's a cat," said Dad. "I can see it's a cat. But where did it come from?"

"I don't know," said James, truthfully.

The little cat came over and sat looking hopefully up at him. James ignored her so she put out a paw and dabbed at his pyjamas.

"Miaow!" she said.

"She seems to know you," said Dad, suspiciously. "Have you seen her before?"

"Well..." said James, slowly. "She's been coming round at breakfast time."

"Ah!" said Dad, looking closely at James. "Maybe she's been coming round for breakfast?"

The cat looked at Dad with wide, golden eyes. "Miaow!" she said, as if she agreed with him.

Dad looked at James with dark, suspicious eyes. "Have you been feeding your breakfast to this cat?" he asked.

8

"I did give her a bit," James admitted.

"So that's why you finished so quickly!" said Dad.

For a moment the kitchen was silent. James looked anxiously at Dad, waiting to see whether he was going to be cross with him. But Dad looked down at the little cat, who blinked her great golden eyes at him and started to purr.

"There's no breakfast ready today, Puss," he said. He turned to James – and he wasn't cross. "You'd better give her a drink of milk to keep her going," he smiled. And he went off upstairs with the tea-tray.

James made himself a bowl of Weetabix, with an extra one for the little cat. But this time he kept the kitchen door closed, so when she finished eating, she settled down in front of the stove and began to wash herself as if she'd come home.

James sat quietly at the table waiting for the others to come and see the cat.

"She might have been left behind when they sold up the farm next door," Mum said. "Poor little creature!"

Jenny sat on the floor, stroking the little cat's head. The little cat purred and snuggled close to her.

"You said we could have a pet when we moved out here," she reminded Mum.

"Well, yes, as soon as we've got settled," said Mum. "But we've hardly unpacked – and the garden's a mess..."

"I did want a puppy," said James. He looked across at the little ginger cat.

Dad groaned. "A puppy needs people around all the time," he said, "and we're away all day." He, too, looked at the cat.

"I wanted a pony," said Jenny. She smiled and went on stroking the cat.

Mum frowned. "A pony needs a stable and a field," she said, watching Jenny's hand smoothing down the ginger fur.

Everyone watched as the cat clambered on to Jenny's lap, turned round three times, and settled down to sleep.

"We haven't chosen a pet," said James, softly, "but a pet seems to have chosen us."

Jenny looked up. "Can we keep her?" she asked.

Dad looked at Mum. Mum looked at Dad. They both stared at the little cat, all curled up now, on Jenny's lap. For a moment the kitchen was quiet except for the purring of the fridge – or was it the purring of the little cat?

"I don't think she belongs to anybody," James said. "She seems to live under the old stone wall across the yard."

"I'll ask around," said Dad. "And if nobody claims her I suppose she'll have to stay here."

"But no more sharing your breakfast with her," Mum told James. "We'll bring some proper cat food back from the supermarket today."

James and his dad went across to the farmhouse to ask the new owners if they'd lost a cat. As soon as the door opened, two great golden dogs leapt out and almost knocked James over. James stepped behind Dad and watched them race off down the garden. Dogs are very bouncy, he thought, nervously.

Dad explained why they'd come.

"Well, as you can see, we have two very lively dogs here. A cat wouldn't stand a chance," the man said. "She probably used to live in your barn – when it *was* a barn."

"I expect that's why she keeps coming back," James said to Dad, as they walked back down to their barn-house.

"She keeps coming back because you keep feeding her," smiled Dad.

"Well, we'll have to keep feeding her,"

said James, "so we might as well keep her."

"You'll have to get a move on in the mornings," Dad warned him. "We have enough to do without waiting for you and the cat to finish eating breakfast!"

"Oh, I will," James promised happily. "I'll eat my breakfast quickly and then feed the cat – honest!"

When Mum and Jenny came back from shopping they brought six tins of cat food with them.

"It's a good job we didn't find a home for the cat," Dad pointed out.

"Well, it was obvious she belonged here once upon a time," said Mum. "She's made herself quite at home."

"So we're going to keep her?" Jenny settled herself on the sofa next to the cat.

"It looks like it," said James. "Nobody else seems to want her."

"Poor Pussy," said Jenny, stroking the cat's ears. "Does nobody want a little stray pussy then?"

"I don't think she's such a poor pussy,"

said Dad. "She's very happy on our sofa."

"Yes, we'll have to get her a basket next," said Mum. "She's not living on the sofa."

"And we'd better get a cat flap," said Dad, "so that she can get in and out while we're away all day."

"And a little collar with her name on it," said James, "in case she gets lost again."

"What name?" asked Jenny.

And they all stopped and looked at each other.

"Ginger?" suggested Mum.

"Too obvious," said James.

"Tabby?" Dad said.

"But she's not!" protested James.

"Dinkie," said Jenny in a soppy little voice.

"Ugh!" said James.

"All right, then, Mr Cleverclogs – what's your suggestion?"

James smiled. "We'll call her Breakfast," he said, "because that's what she came for."

Breakfast opened her little pink mouth and yawned and stretched, then settled into the sofa cushion and went back to sleep. She had obviously come to stay!

Chapter 2

Breakfast was very happy in her new home and Jenny and James were very happy with their new pet, even though she was neither pony nor puppy!

"We'll go to the DIY stores on the ring road," said Dad, next day. "I'll buy a cat flap and fit it in the kitchen door. Then Breakfast can go in and out while we're all away."

"We ought to take her to the vet," said Mum. "Don't suppose she's had her jabs. I'll make an appointment for Monday evening when we all get back home."

So Dad and Jenny worked all Sunday morning to fit the cat flap on the back door and James spent a great deal of Sunday afternoon teaching Breakfast how to use it. He lay down on the floor in front of the door and showed Breakfast how to knock the flap open.

"There you are," he said, holding it wide open. "Now you can climb through."

But Breakfast merely yawned in a bored sort of way and stalked off across the yard.

"You'll have to bribe her," said Mum passing by with a wheelbarrow full of old stones. "There's a bit of old cheese in the fridge."

So James fetched the cheese, broke a piece off and held it out through the cat flap.

"Come on, Breakfast!" he called. "Here's some food for you."

Breakfast came running down the path, stopped at the door, shot a paw out, and neatly flicked the cheese from James's hand. Surprised, James pulled back his hand and the cat flap dropped and hit his fingers.

"Ow!" he said.

Now Breakfast sat outside, happily licking her paws, and James sat inside, rubbing his sore fingers.

"She'll never get the hang of it," he moaned.

"Push her through to show her how it works," said Dad, on his way out to unload Mum's stones. "But do it gently!"

"I'll sit inside," said Jenny. "You go out, then she's got somebody to help her on both sides."

It sounded a good idea. James gave the lump of cheese to Jenny, opened the kitchen door and stepped outside. But before he could close the door again Breakfast slid past and sat inside, looking at Jenny hopefully. Jenny laughed and gave her a bit of cheese.

"Don't do that; she hasn't learned her lesson yet," said James.

"No, but she was clever, wasn't she?" laughed Jenny. "She deserves a reward."

"Well, you've got the cat – you try shoving her outside to me," said James, closing the door firmly.

So Jenny opened the cat flap and posted Breakfast through the hole.

"Wiouw!" moaned Breakfast, crossly. But she stood in front of James, waiting for her reward.

"Now push a bit of cheese through," said James. "She's earned it."

They played this game until there was no more cheese left and Breakfast seemed to have got the hang of climbing through the flap. She wasn't so good at opening it, though – when they left her outside she sat miaowing pitifully until Jenny opened the kitchen door and let her in.

"She'll soon learn to use the flap when we're not in," said Mum.

"But I bet when we *are* in she'll make us open the door for her," laughed James.

On Monday morning James was first downstairs for once. He went across to the new cat basket – but Breakfast wasn't there!

"Jenny, she's gone!" he called. "Breakfast's run away!"

"She'll be back," said Mum, coming into the kitchen. "She's probably only gone out to investigate my new garden."

Sure enough, by the time they were all sitting down to breakfast there came a little moan from the other side of the door.

"I'll open it," said Jenny, getting up.

"She ought to use her own door,"

grumbled Dad. "After all the time it took me to fix it!"

"She'll use it when we're out," smiled Mum. "Now, come on, James, eat up quickly and then you can feed the cat."

It was odd how everyone was ready on time yet nobody had been rushing around. Even James ate quickly so that he had time to feed Breakfast before they had to leave. As soon as she finished she went back to her place under the old stone wall.

"Bye, Breakfast!" called James as he ran down the lane to the bus-stop. "Don't forget you can use your cat flap to get back into the house."

"And don't forget we're taking you to the vet's this evening," said Jenny.

Mum had bought a carrying box to take Breakfast up to the vet's. Breakfast hated being shut up in it – she screeched and scratched. Jenny and James sat on the back seat of the car, holding firmly on to the box.

"It's a good job we're not going far," said Dad. "She'd soon eat her way out of that prison."

"Shhh, Breakfast!" crooned Jenny, through the air holes in the box. "Soon be there."

But even when they got to the vet's they had to stay in the waiting-room until it was their turn. All the time they sat there Breakfast scrabbled and scratched at the carrying box. All the other patients seemed to be dogs, and they were very interested in the strange noises coming from the cat box. They whined and sniffed and yelped and barked – one even set up a terrible howling. For once, James was quite glad they hadn't got a dog.

At last they were called into the surgery.

"Hello, I'm Rachel," said the vet, pulling on a fresh pair of plastic gloves. "What have you brought for me?"

So Dad explained how Breakfast came to live with them.

"I expect she's been living almost wild since the farm was sold," said Rachel. "When you moved in she soon realized she was on to a good thing!"

Rachel lifted a very angry cat out of the box. Breakfast's fur was standing on end, her little pink mouth was spitting and snarling, her teeth snatching at anything in their way.

But Rachel didn't seem to mind. "Whoops! Steady, little cat!" she said, settling her down on the table. "Now, let's give you a check-up before we decide on your jabs."

Rachel held the cat down on the table and felt all round her back and tummy, looked into her mouth and eyes and touched her nose.

"Well, she's very healthy just now," she said, "but I'll bet she's never had a vaccination in her little life so I think we'd better give her one right away. Would you like to hold her?" She turned to James.

James hesitated. But before he could refuse, Breakfast had jumped up on to his chest, pushed her claws into his sweatshirt and buried her head into his neck.

"Just hold her underneath – that's right," Rachel said. "So long as I can get at her neck fur..." She took the syringe the assistant passed her and plunged it into Breakfast's neck. "There! She didn't feel a thing," she assured James, who had turned his head away. "That's the spare flesh her mother used to carry her by – it's not sensitive."

Even so, James stroked Breakfast and cuddled her close.

Rachel pulled off her plastic gloves and threw them into the waste bin. "It's just as well to get that done before she has her kittens," she said casually.

There was a moment's silence.

"Kittens?" said Dad.

"What kittens?" asked Mum.

Rachel looked from one to the other. "Oh, didn't you know?" she smiled. "She'll be having kittens in a week or two."

There was a moment's silence in the surgery. Mum and Dad looked grimly at the cat, still clinging to James's chest. James suddenly felt nervous, as if he was holding a great and precious burden. He tucked his arm tighter under Breakfast's rump.

But Jenny grinned. "That's great!" she exclaimed. "How many will she have?"

Rachel shrugged. "It's too early to tell," she said. "But she's a small cat, and very young, so maybe not more than three or four."

"Three or four!" repeated Dad, dismayed.

"What are we going to do with three or four cats around the house?" asked Mum. "We're out all day during the week."

"Oh, she'll look after them herself for the first week or two, don't you worry," said Rachel. "And once they're old enough you can find homes for them."

"How?" asked Dad, gloomily.

"You can advertise on our notice-board out in the waiting-room," said Rachel. "And I'm sure the children will pass the word around their friends at school."

James looked at Jenny. Jenny winked at James. They both knew they had no intention of passing the word around – not just yet. After all, they'd been wanting a pet for ages. Now they could have one each and a few over!

Chapter 3

Breakfast didn't seem very worried at the prospect of becoming a mother. She slept under her wall when the family was out and came running up to the door as soon as they arrived home, waiting for them to open it. She ate all her food, drank lots of milk, and grew fatter by the day. But she was always ready for a game with Jenny or a cuddle with James.

But if Breakfast wasn't worried, the rest of the family was. James and Jenny went to the school library and took out several books about cats and kittens. Mum called at the bookshop and bought a paperback on rearing kittens.

"You're all making too much fuss," said Dad. "Any self-respecting cat can deal with it all herself without your help."

Next day, he called at the pet shop and picked up several leaflets about pregnant cats and their kittens.

A week later they were all experts.

"I'll put her on cod-liver oil and extra vitamins," Mum said.

"I'll clear a cupboard out in case she wants to go in there to have her kittens," said Jenny.

"I'm going to make a birthing box," announced James, looking up from his latest cat book.

"A what?"

"Birthing box – a place for Breakfast to have her kittens in. The plans are here." James peered at a page full of diagrams. "I'll need to use your bench, Dad – and borrow some tools."

"Sorry," said Dad. "I've left most of my tools down at the workshop in town and I haven't set up a bench in the outhouse yet."

"You can use an ordinary cardboard box," said Mum, looking over James's shoulder at the book. "Cut the front off, fit it into the bottom of the cupboard, fill it with newspapers and there you are – one birthing box."

"But I wanted to carve it – you know, like a baby's cradle." James loved making things, the more complicated the better.

"Not much point – they'll be out of it in a couple of weeks," said Mum.

"If they ever get into it," said Dad, waving a leaflet about. "It says here she'll probably go off outside to have the kittens in private."

"Oh, no! We need to watch her in case anything goes wrong!" said Jenny.

"Nothing will go wrong," Dad assured her. "Having kittens is as easy as shelling peas for a cat."

"Shelling peas would be impossible for a cat," James pointed out.

"Well, easy as unravelling the bottom of Mum's sweater," laughed Dad. He pointed to the back of Mum's chair where Breakfast was busily tugging at a long, dangling thread.

Mum turned. "Oh Breakfast, you naughty cat – that's my new sweater! Get off!"

But Breakfast couldn't get off – the thread was tangled in her claws. Jenny got down on the floor and wove it in and out until Breakfast's claws came free.

"Miawow!" spat Breakfast, shooting off across the kitchen and out through the open door.

"If that's the way a grown cat behaves, just think of the fun we're going to have with four or five kittens," laughed Dad.

"Oh, don't remind me," groaned Mum. "What are we going to do with them all?"

"Don't worry," said James. "The book says Breakfast will take good care of them all by herself for the first week or two."

"It's not the first week or two that's the problem," said Mum. "We'll have to keep them for at least six weeks. Think of the mess in the kitchen!"

"They can live in the utility room," Dad suggested.

"I'll clear the bottom of the airing cupboard so that Breakfast can practise going in there," said Jenny, going across to open the utility room door.

"And when you've finished, I'll put my birthing box in place just to get her used to it." James rushed off after her.

"As soon as they're born, I'll put a litter tray down in the utility room, so that Breakfast can train them to use it," said Mum.

"You see? All it takes is a bit of organization," said Dad. "They won't get into mischief in the utility room."

"Want to bet?" grinned James. Dad was great at organization, but James had a feeling that kittens had never heard of the word.

One Saturday morning a couple of weeks later, James came downstairs and called Breakfast in from the garden. He stood by the door, peering out into the misty rain, and called and called and called, but Breakfast didn't come.

"Breakfast's missing," he told Jenny, who was shuffling around in her dressing-gown.

"She'll be out in the garden," said Jenny.

"No, it's raining again and you know how she hates getting wet."

Now they both stood at the kitchen door, calling out into the rain. But Breakfast never came.

"It's no good," said Jenny, "we'll just have to go and look for her. I'll go and get dressed while you sort out the cagoules and wellies."

"Where are they?"

"Where you left them, I expect."

"No, we haven't worn them since we moved in. Where did Mum decide we should keep them?"

"Oh – in the utility room, of course. Cagoules on the back of the door, wellies under the sink."

"The sooner Dad builds us a porch, the better," grumbled James, as he padded across the kitchen. "We can't keep all our outdoor stuff in there much longer. Every time we need anything we'll disturb our kittens."

"Not yet we won't – and you certainly won't disturb Breakfast this morning," Jenny said grimly.

But she was wrong on both counts.

As soon as he opened the door to the utility room, James knew something was happening. He could hear some thin, high squeaks and a single deep purring. That was Breakfast, he knew. She must be hiding in her box – at last! He crouched down and peered across the room into the airing cupboard. The door was always left open so that Breakfast could get used to going in and out as she pleased, though she'd never been inside since Jenny put the box in. And she wasn't in there now. Where on earth could she have got to?

James stood up and gazed around the little room. He could hear her purring but it wasn't coming from the airing cupboard, he realized now – it was coming from the worktop across the other side of the room. James's eyes followed the sound – and saw Breakfast lying on a pile of dirty towels in the laundry basket, purring away.

"Oh, there you are, Breakfast!" said James, cheerfully. "It's no use settling down in there – we're washing today..."

But Breakfast didn't even look up at him. She just turned her back on him and James saw that she was licking something on her tummy. Breakfast often licked her tummy when she washed herself, but this didn't seem to be the same, James decided. The licking was more frantic, somehow, as if it were more important, more vital... Suddenly James stopped and stared hard into the basket. Breakfast was still purring deeply, and still licking short, hard licks – not her tummy, this time, but something close up to her...

"Wow!" breathed James. "A kitten!"

He was about to call Jenny, but then he remembered what his cat book had said about not disturbing the mother cat at this time. If she was frightened she might even kill the kittens rather than have them hurt. Slowly, carefully, James stood up and backed into the kitchen. Then he closed the utility room door very quietly. He stood by the door, thinking hard. If Breakfast was going to have all her kittens in the laundry basket, on last week's towels, Mum was not going to be pleased. On the other hand, they mustn't be moved. So what were they going to do?

"What's all this about Breakfast going missing?" boomed Dad, coming into the kitchen with the early-morning tea-tray.

"Shhh!" hissed James, pointing in the direction of the utility room.

"What?"

"She's in there," he said.

"Oh, that's all right then," said Dad, plonking the tray down with a crash.

James winced at the noise. "She's in the laundry basket," he hissed.

"Not for long, she isn't," said Dad. "Washing today, you know." He tipped the tea mugs noisily into the kitchen sink.

"I know," said James, desperately. "I've been thinking about that."

"I'm glad to hear it. Time you gave me a hand," smiled Dad.

"But, you see, there's Breakfast—"

"Well, we can get a load into the machine, then have breakfast while it washes."

"Not breakfast as in food," said James, impatiently. "*Breakfast* – our cat!"

"Oh, I see." Dad leaned against the sink and looked at James. "Well, all right – we'll leave her in the laundry basket for now."

"I think we'll have to leave her longer than that," said James. "She's just having her kittens in it."

Dad turned. "In the laundry basket? You mean...?"

James nodded. "Yes, she's having them right now. I saw the first one and then I left her to it."

"Right – we'll leave her in peace this morning," said Dad. "Though I don't know what Mum's going to say about the towels and the basket."

Just then Jenny rushed in, pulling a sweater over her head.

"What are you standing about for, James?" she called. "Where's my cagoule and the wellies?" She made a move towards the utility room door.

"Stop!" said Dad, holding up an arm to bar her way.

Jenny skidded to a halt. "Have you found her, then?"

"She's in the utility room," smiled Dad.

"Oh, good. I'll just go and see her—"

"No!" cried James. He lowered his voice. "She's having her kittens," he explained.

Jenny stared. "How do you know?"

"I saw the first one just after it was born."

"Wow!" Jenny gave a little squeal of excitement.

"Shhhh!" said Dad and James together.

"Is she in the airing cupboard?" Jenny asked softly.

James grinned. "No, she isn't," he said. "Seems she prefers the laundry basket to my box."

"And I spent ages cleaning that cupboard out!" said Jenny, indignantly. "Is she all right?"

James nodded. "She seemed to be quite happy," he said. "I heard her purring and the little kitten squeaked."

When Mum came down they told her the news.

"So you see, you can't have your basket back for a week or two," said Dad.

Mum didn't mind. She went straight to the utility room door and peeped in.

"Three now," she said, her eyes shining. "And all feeding nicely."

They ate breakfast in silence. Everyone was listening hard for any sounds coming from the utility room, but they couldn't hear anything. After breakfast, they tiptoed around the kitchen; even Dad tried to clear the dishes very gently.

"I'll peep in – just to make sure she's managing," he said. "Then we'll leave her in peace."

"Can't we have a look?" pleaded Jenny. "She won't notice us – we're smaller than you."

"And quieter," grinned James, backing

away as Dad flicked him with the tea towel.

"Well, so long as you stay by the door and don't make any move towards the basket," her mother warned. "If Breakfast panics she might harm the kittens."

Jenny and James crouched by the door and peered across the room. The laundry basket stood on the worktop at the far end. It was a woven cane basket, with handles and steep sides, just right for a family of cats, but not much good for viewing.

"Breakfast's got her back to us," Jenny complained. "I can't see any kittens."

"Move round to the side a bit," said James. "Look past Breakfast, right under her tummy. She's still cleaning one of them."

Now Jenny looked more carefully. "Oh, yes!" she whispered. "I see now. They're not little fluffy things at all – just damp and smooth, and smaller than my hand."

They both stood at the door, scarcely breathing for fear of disturbing Breakfast and her kittens. It was so quiet now that they could even hear the sound of Breakfast's rough tongue rubbing the newest kitten's fur and the tiny squeaks of the others, nuzzling under their mother.

"Eating their Breakfast," whispered James.

Jenny laughed softly at the joke. "Hey – how many can you see?" she suddenly asked.

James looked hard at the tiny creatures, scarcely cats at all, suckling up to Breakfast. "One, two ... three," he counted.

"And the one she's still cleaning," Jenny reminded him.

"That makes four." James looked at Jenny and grinned. "I wonder if that's the last?"

Chapter 4

Jenny and James stood at the door hardly daring to breath while Breakfast nudged the fourth kitten up to join the rest of them. For a while there was not a sound in the utility room as the kittens nuzzled close and apparently fell asleep.

"Come on," Jenny whispered. "We'd better leave them now." She tiptoed away into the kitchen.

James was about to follow when he heard an odd sound. At first he thought it was a fly, buzzing at the window, then, as it grew louder, he decided it might be a wasp or a bee, drawn out of hibernation by the warm sunshine which now flooded the room. Well, they didn't want flies or wasps buzzing around the newly-born kittens. James stepped carefully into the room and looked up at the window. But there was no fly, no wasp, even though he could hear the noise getting louder and louder. And now he recognized it for what it was – not a buzzing at all, but a deep purring sound, coming from the basket.

Breakfast is singing to her kittens, thought James, and he couldn't resist another peep – which was how he saw that another kitten was just being born!

James stood by, holding his breath, afraid to move in case he disturbed Breakfast, afraid to stay in case he disturbed the kittens. He needn't have worried: Breakfast was far too busy to notice him, and the kittens were far too sleepy.

Especially the fifth kitten, which didn't seem to be moving at all. Breakfast licked and licked until it was quite clean and smooth and damp, but it didn't respond like the others had. James watched anxiously. What if it never moved? It would get cold out there, away from its mother's fur. And it would starve unless it crawled close to her teats.

The same idea seemed to have occurred to Breakfast. She stopped licking and nudged the kitten with her nose. It rolled over a little way but only because she'd pushed it. Now she sniffed at it, almost as if she wasn't sure it was hers, but still it didn't move. James peered as closely as he dared. And then he had a shock.

The fifth kitten wasn't one single kitten. Now that Breakfast had nudged them apart, he could see two kittens!

"The fifth *and* the sixth!" breathed James. "Born together – they must be twins!"

For a moment he smiled. Of course all the kittens were part of the same litter – sextuplets, he supposed they were. But these little two had clung so tightly together, even as they'd been born, that he felt sure they were more twinned than the rest of them. He looked more closely at the smooth tiny creatures, and stopped smiling.

He couldn't be sure, but it seemed to him that the twin kittens weren't even breathing. Oh, help! They'd have to call Rachel, but by the time she got right out here, the kittens might be...

James blinked hard. And when he'd cleared the tears from his eyes he saw Breakfast had picked up one of the twin kittens by the scruff of its neck and was shaking it gently, to and fro, to and fro.

Like Grandad's watch, thought James. Grandad had an old pocket watch which had belonged to *his* dad, who had been an engine driver on the railways. It was a very good watch but sometimes it stopped and Grandad took it in the palm of his hand and rocked it to get it started.

"To get it started..." muttered James, eyes fixed on the tiny damp creature in Breakfast's mouth. "Oh, get started, please!"

He held his breath and watched wide-eyed as a great shiver ran right through the little kitten's body. Breakfast must have felt it too, for she put it gently down among the others, nosing them aside to shove it up to a free teat. The new kitten raised its head, blindly, and James could even see its tiny pink mouth trembling as it searched for its food. But would it find any? And even if it did, would it have enough strength to suck?

Breakfast didn't stop to find out; she turned her attention to the other twin and gave it the same treatment – swinging it gently to and fro, then snuggling it amongst her belly fur.

James was longing to help the new kittens along a bit but he knew he mustn't interfere – one touch from him and Breakfast might reject them both. And those tiny twins would need a lot of attention from their mother if they were going to thrive. He stood there clenching his hands tight, partly from anxiety and partly to stop them reaching out to help. He knew he could do nothing except stand very still and watch. Breakfast turned her head and gave the twin kittens another firm nudge – first one, then the other. They shivered slightly – and then opened their tiny mouths and clamped on to a couple of teats.

James let out a huge sigh of relief, and it seemed to him that Breakfast did, too. He couldn't see whether the twin kittens were feeding or not, but Breakfast suddenly glared at him, as if to say, *Go away now! You can leave it all to me*. She curled herself closer to all the kittens and started her loud, rhythmic purring noise. She seemed to think everything was all right, thought James. He walked silently out of the room and gently closed the door behind him.

"You've been in there disturbing the kittens," Jenny accused him.

"No, I haven't," he said. "I've been doing something far more interesting than that."

Jenny stared at him. "You didn't move them into your box, did you?"

"No, of course not."

"So what were you doing?"

"I was just watching the rest of them being born," said James, casually.

"Some more?" Jenny squealed. "Why didn't you call me?"

"That would have disturbed them," James pointed out.

"Yes, well, I suppose it would have," Jenny agreed. "How many?"

James smiled. "Just the two."

"Wow! That makes six altogether. Dad'll have a fit!"

"I suppose these last two could count as one," said James.

"What do you mean?"

"Well, they were born at exactly the same time, sort of clinging together. I thought they were just one kitten at first—"

"You're sure there were two?" asked Jenny.

James nodded. "Oh, yes. Breakfast licked them until they fell apart. I think they're twins, you see."

Jenny frowned. "I don't see how they can be. They were all born at the same time, so they're sextuplets."

"No, quadruplets," James corrected her. "The first four and then those last two twins."

"Never mind the arithmetic, are they all right?"

"Well, Breakfast had to shake them to get them going."

"Shake them?" Jenny looked horrified. "She might have killed them."

"Killed who?" asked Mum, dumping a load of dirty laundry on to the kitchen table. "I shall be glad when those four kittens can be moved out of my laundry basket."

"Six," said James. "Breakfast had twins after you'd gone."

"Twins? Oh, goodness! That makes seven cats in the house now. What on earth are we going to do with them?"

"The question is, what on earth are you going to do with that lot?" asked James, pointing at the heap of clothes on the table.

"Wash it, of course," said Mum. "Unless you want to put it in."

"In where?" asked James

"In the machine. Where else?"

But James suddenly dashed to the door of the utility room and spread-eagled himself right across it.

"Over my dead body!" he said.

"Don't be ridiculous, James," said his mother, sorting out the dirty clothes into

50

piles. "We've got to do our washing, kittens or no kittens."

"But you can't switch the washing-machine on," Jenny protested. "You'll upset the kittens."

"So how am I going to do the washing?" asked Mum.

Silence. Everyone stared anxiously at the heap of washing on the table. Dad, coming into the kitchen just then, followed their gaze.

"What's the matter?" he asked. "Have my socks walked out on their own?"

Nobody laughed. Mum looked up and raised her eyebrows. James glared across from the utility room door.

"She can't do the washing in the utility room, can she, Dad?" Jenny burst out. "Not with the kittens in there."

"Ah," said Dad. "I see the problem."

"We all see the problem," said Mum, rather sharply. "What's the solution?"

"Funny you should ask that," Dad grinned. "It's a good job I collected all those leaflets – there's one specially about rearing kittens. Hang on."

He went across the hall to his office, where the family computer was kept, and came back with a handful of leaflets.

"Right. Let's see what the experts say..." he mumbled to himself as he quickly scanned the page. "Yes, I knew it was here somewhere." He looked around the kitchen. "Come on, James, get away from that door — nobody's going to harm those four kittens."

"Six," James corrected, as he reluctantly came over to the table. "Breakfast's just had twins."

Dad raised his eyes to the ceiling. "What's the record for a litter?" he said to Mum. "Ten? A dozen?"

"Never mind counting kittens," said Mum, "just find out what we're to do about the washing."

Dad looked at the leaflet. "It says here that the kittens aren't aware of anything much except their mother's voice until they're a couple of weeks old."

Mum breathed a sigh of relief. "By which time they'll have got used to the sound of the machine," she said, gathering up a bundle of socks. "Come on, James. You're so concerned about the kittens, you can be in charge of the washing from now on."

Jenny laughed as James gathered up a heap of shirts.

"Well, this way I get to see the kittens," he reminded her.

"So you do!" Jenny grabbed the remainder of the washing and followed him into the utility room.

As they loaded the machine, James kept looking across to the laundry basket up on its worktop, but there was no movement, not even from Breakfast.

"She's fast asleep," whispered Jenny, "and all the kittens too."

"She must be exhausted," said Mum. "We'll leave a bowl of milk for her as soon as we've got the washing on."

Mum turned the knob to the right programme then switched on the machine. Jenny and James stuck their fingers in their ears and looked anxiously across at the cat family but nobody stirred, even when the machine started up.

"Crisis over," smiled Mum. "Now, come on, let's get that milk."

After that, nobody worried about the noise from the machines or from the kitchen. Next morning, Breakfast came to greet them as usual, lapped up her food and a great deal of water, and then went over to the door to be let out.

"How will she ever teach her kittens to use the cat flap if she never uses it herself?" asked James.

"Oh, that's not her problem," said Dad, opening the door for Breakfast.

"Why not?"

"Well, they won't need a cat flap until they go to their new homes," he said.

James stopped eating his toast. Jenny stopped drinking her tea.

"Which new homes?" asked James.

"Oh, we'll find them homes, right enough," said Dad, easily. "I'll ask around at work, you ask around in school."

"Yes, you might make some new friends that way," said Mum. "You can invite them over to see the kittens."

"They might even want to choose one for themselves," added Dad, hopefully.

"But only if their parents come too," said Mum. "Don't go offering the kittens to just anyone."

As their parents went on discussing the problem of finding homes for the kittens, James sat silently scowling at the honey pot and Jenny looked deep into her cup. So far neither of them had even mentioned the kittens to anyone at school; they had no intention of inviting anyone to "choose one for themselves".

As far as James and Jenny were concerned, the six kittens belonged to Breakfast – and to them.

Chapter 5

Breakfast soon made it quite clear that she was in charge of her kittens. She didn't mind people coming in and out of the utility room, but if they ventured too close to the little nest in the basket she hissed loudly to warn them off. So there was no question of using the laundry basket – not for the next few weeks, at least.

On Monday evening, Dad produced a bulky plastic bag from the car boot.

"Present for you," he said to Mum. "Happy kittens' birthday!"

"For me?" Mum was delighted – she loved surprises. She was a little less delighted when she saw what it was.

"Oh, great! A new laundry basket." She pulled a face and laughed. "That's not a present for me – it's for whoever does the washing."

"It's really for Breakfast and the kittens," said James. "Now they can settle into their new home quite happily."

"They seemed happy enough to me when I put fresh kitchen paper into their little nest," smiled Mum. "And talking of homes, have you found anyone interested in taking one of the kittens yet?"

Jenny and James exchanged glances.

"Not yet," said Jenny.

"Later," said James.

Dad was silent.

"What about you?" Mum asked him. "Anyone at work interested in a kitten?"

"Well..." Dad looked thoughtful. "You know my workshops are close to the old canal?"

They all nodded. Dad was a carpenter who made beautiful furniture. His workshop was in an old converted warehouse, along with those of several other artists and craftsmen.

"The weavers in the back rooms are having terrible trouble with mice nesting in their sacks of wool, nibbling at the yarn and splitting it..."

"So they need a kitten?" asked Mum, eagerly.

"Well, they don't want one just for themselves. Their idea is that it would have the run of the whole place – keep the mice down like the old farm cats used to do; like Breakfast did in the barns."

"That's a bit tough on a little kitten," said James, indignantly.

"I'll bet Breakfast used to enjoy it," Dad pointed out.

"But who would look after it?" asked Jenny. "You're not there at the weekends, are you?"

"No, but Carol is." Carol was Dad's assistant, a student who was learning to work with wood. "She's just moved into one of the studios under the roof and she's delighted at the idea of having a cat."

"But it will miss all its brothers and sisters," moaned James.

"It will miss them anyway," Dad pointed out. "They can't all go together to the same home."

"Unless..." Mum paused and looked at Dad.

"Unless what?" James asked hopefully. Maybe she was going to suggest they keep them all together here, in their barn-home.

"Unless Dad took two of them to the warehouse?" Mum smiled her best, charming smile at Dad. "I'm sure there are enough mice to keep two cats fully employed."

"And they'd be company for each other," said Jenny, suddenly excited by the idea. "You could let them have those two that James calls the twins."

"Well, I'll have to ask Carol how she feels about it," said Dad.

"And don't you forget to ask around, too." Mum looked hard at Jenny and James.

Jenny and James said nothing.

They said nothing at school, either, but they reckoned without the countryside bush telegraph.

Their bus-stop was the start of the school run and the bus was usually waiting for them, with one or two older pupils already aboard, sitting apart in their early morning silence. Neither Jenny nor James knew any of the others so they always sat together, feeling rather awkward and shy. But one morning the bus was late and people were standing around, some chatting, some staring gloomily and silently ahead.

"What happens if we're late for school?" James asked anxiously. In spite of being such a slow starter in the mornings, he hated being late for anything – especially school.

The girl in front turned round and smiled.

"It'll be all right," she assured them. "The driver will have phoned into school. We won't get a late mark. After all, it's not our fault, is it?"

"No," Jenny agreed eagerly. "What do you think has happened?"

The girl shrugged. "I'll bet it's broken down coming up Slack Hill," she said. "Some of the old buses just can't make it, especially in the winter."

"What happens then?" asked James, already worrying about next winter.

"If we're lucky, and if the weather's really bad, we go back home." The girl turned to face them. "You two live in the new barn conversion up at Butterfield Farm, don't you?"

She told them her name was Rosie Burford and that she lived in an old cottage down the valley. She was in the Upper School, a year ahead of Jenny, which was why they hadn't seen her around school. Jenny introduced herself, then, as an afterthought, her brother, James.

"So how are your kittens getting on?" Rosie asked him.

"How did you know we had some kittens?" he asked, wide-eyed.

"My uncle lives up in the old farmhouse near you – he's got a couple of golden Labradors. Do you know him?"

"Oh, yes," said James, with some exaggeration. "His dogs are very bouncy."

Rosie laughed. "They are that!" she agreed. "But they're lovely all the same. I wish I could have one," she added wistfully.

"Why don't you?" asked Jenny, eager to keep the conversation flowing. She was glad that Rosie had spoken to them; she'd often given a friendly smile as they boarded the bus, as if inviting Jenny to sit with her.

But now Rosie was frowning sadly. "Our old dog died last year and now Mum's got a job again, we can't really have a puppy at home all day on its own."

"Yes, that's what my dad said." Jenny smiled sympathetically. Then, on an impulse, she added, "But cats don't need company all day..."

James turned bright red and stuck her hard in the ribs with his finger.

"What was that for?" she asked.

"Not a word," muttered James, out of the side of his mouth. "We agreed—"

"What's he saying?" asked Rosie.

"Oh, nothing," said Jenny carelessly. "Look – here's the bus, at last!"

The two girls got on the bus and this time they sat together. James stumped angrily after them and sat right behind Jenny, so that he could tug her hair if she made any further mention of cats or kittens. But the girls were deep into horses now. Apparently Rosie had a pony in a field close by and spent her weekends helping out at the stables in the next village. Jenny was agog.

"I get to ride most weekends," said Rosie. "Why don't you come with me one Saturday?"

By the time they arrived at school, Jenny and Rosie were devoted friends, and James stumped off to lessons haunted by the suspicion that one of Breakfast's kittens would soon be exchanged for pony rides.

If Dad took the "twins" to the warehouse and Jenny turned traitor and offered another to Rosie, they would've got rid of three kittens even before they'd opened their eyes, James calculated, gloomily. And that was without Mum's determined efforts, and James knew all about those. Mum could organize global warfare if she set her mind to it; finding homes for a couple of kittens would be child's play to her.

But so far, it seemed, she wasn't having any success, James noted with relief that evening. On the other hand, Dad's student, Carol, was thrilled to hear about the "twins", and Jenny talked endlessly about her new friend Rosie and her horses.

"She knew all about our kittens," Jenny told Mum. "I've invited her over to see them."

"I'd have to talk to her mother before she takes one home," said Mum, firmly.

"And it's too soon for anyone to see them," added James. "They all look the same just now."

But by the next weekend this was no longer true. Peering into the basket, James could just make out their different markings: a couple of very dark ones with paler markings – tabbies, maybe – a gingery one like Breakfast herself, and one with such pale fur it hardly showed up at all. The twin kittens – the weakest, the smallest, and the slowest to change – were still sleek and smooth as baby otters; there was no telling how they'd turn out. James called them the Tiny Twins because they were so small, and because he knew they had been born together.

Although the kittens' eyes were still closed tight, they could scuttle and shift around Breakfast's tummy, pushing and shoving each other out of the way until the laundry basket seemed to bulge with bodies.

"What if it tips over?" James asked Dad, as they watched the kittens scrambling blindly about one morning.

"I don't think they're strong enough for that," said Dad. "But it's going to be a bit of a squash as they go on growing."

"We'll have to get a bigger basket," suggested James.

Dad groaned. "I've already bought a new laundry basket," he pointed out.

"You should have bought the next size up," grinned James, "then they could move house when they get too big for this one."

"At that rate we'd need a new basket every week," Dad pointed out. "No, I think we'll leave the housing problem to Breakfast — she'll know what to do."

Breakfast no longer stayed with the kittens all the time; she often went outside to sit on her old wall in the sunshine, as if to take a little break from kitten-rearing.

"I know how she feels," laughed Mum. "I could do with a break from mothering you lot!"

"We'll need a break very soon," Dad

pointed out. "Life's going to be very hectic when those kittens get moving."

"I can't wait," said James, with feeling. Not only had Breakfast made it quite clear she needed no help with her kittens, but Jenny was off down the field to see Rosie and her horse most evenings now and he was feeling a bit left out of things.

But he didn't have to wait long before the kittens, at least, needed him.

The best moment of James's day was when he got home from school. As soon as the kitchen door opened, Breakfast came running to greet him and he'd sit on the floor, stroking and cuddling her as she nuzzled up to him, purring loudly. This was their own special routine every afternoon.

"James, change out of your school uniform before you let Breakfast crawl all over you!" Jenny reminded him every afternoon.

And as if she understood Jenny's complaint, Breakfast would jump off James's lap and run out through the kitchen door, leaving James to run upstairs to change out of his school clothes.

But that afternoon James was disappointed – Breakfast didn't come running to greet him at all.

"She'll be feeding the kittens or something," Jenny said carelessly. She was about to rush off to Bottom Field to see Rosie's horse. Kittens came second to horses with Jenny.

But James was worried – it wasn't like Breakfast to hide away when they came home. Thoughtfully, he walked across the kitchen and peered through the utility room door.

"Breakfast?" he called softly, looking across the room to the basket. And then he stopped, his eyes big with shock. There was no sign of Breakfast – and no sign of her kittens, either!

The basket was quite empty. It was tipped over and the lining of old towels trailed out on the floor. James stood quite still, listening to the thump of his heartbeat, feeling his palms go cold and clammy. He remembered Mum's warnings about mother cats who killed their kittens if they thought they were in danger. Was that what Breakfast had done? Was it all his fault, going in and out too often?

James took a shaky, sobbing breath and clung on to the edge of the door, feeling sick and dizzy. All those tiny kittens – and his beautiful Breakfast – where had they gone? He gazed down blindly at the upturned basket ... and suddenly became aware of movement amongst the heap of towels. Something was hiding in there; something was squeaking...

James took a couple of steps towards the basket, then he paused. Had Breakfast left one kitten behind? Should he rescue it? But if he did, how could they rear it, with no mother to feed from? He opened his mouth to call for Mum, but his voice was weak and wobbly and, anyway, Mum was still out at the car, unpacking a load of new plants. And Jenny was no use – her mind was full of horses.

Even as he stood there dithering, Breakfast suddenly appeared, stalking along the tiled floor as if she was very busy just then. James had no idea where she'd come from but as she passed him he automatically bent to stroke her, as usual. But Breakfast didn't even look up at him, didn't stop to purr, didn't wait for a cuddle. Stepping lightly across the room, tail wafting proudly, she made her way to the heap of towels.

"Oh, no!" James breathed. Was she going to kill that last little kitten?

But Breakfast didn't kill it. She picked it up by the scruff of its neck and carried it across the room, past the dithering, trembling James, past the door – and into the bottom of the airing cupboard, where she dropped it into the birthing box. Then she turned to look back at James, as if to make sure he'd noted the change of address, climbed into the box, curled herself round her kittens and settled in.

Now James could hear the familiar squeaks and squawks coming from the cupboard – far too many and far too loud for the single kitten he'd just seen. It was the kittens shifting themselves into position ready for teatime. Of course Breakfast hadn't killed her kittens! She'd just moved them to roomier premises.

"Clever cat!" whispered James. He peered cautiously into the airing cupboard, just to make sure they were all settled in their new home.

And then he saw a pair of tiny, shiny eyes peering out from under Breakfast's fur – kitten eyes. And there was another pair – and another! Seething with excitement, James backed away and ran outside.

"Mum!" he called. "Mum, the kittens have opened their eyes."

"Oh dear!" said Mum. "Now we'll have to keep *our* eyes open – they'll be on the move any time now."

"Oh, they're on the move already," laughed James. "They've even moved house!"

After supper, when Jenny had at last stopped raving on about Rosie's pony, James told her all about the kittens' new home and they went over to inspect it. But instead of looking at a box full of kittens they were faced with what seemed like a room full of wriggling, squirming animals, clambering out of their box to slide and slither on the tiled floor. They were like tiny soft toys with rag legs too floppy to support them. But they were obviously excited by their new game, leaving several little puddles on the floor to prove it.

"We'll have to put a litter tray out for them now," said Dad.

"They can have a seed tray from the yard," said Mum. "I'll fill it up with cat litter."

"Well, at least you can have the laundry basket back again, Mum," smiled Jenny.

"Perhaps you should take it," smiled Mum. "You make more washing than the rest of us put together."

"You'll have to be careful doing the

washing," said James anxiously. "You might tread on one of them."

"Or even put one in the wash," grinned Jenny.

"Don't even think of it," said James, horrified. "Just keep a lookout for them, that's all."

"We'll have to keep a lookout all the time," sighed Mum. "Heavens knows what they'll get up to once their legs grow stronger!"

Dad was watching Breakfast round up her kittens.

"That's funny," he said. "There's only four here – where are the other two?"

Everyone looked round the room – except James, who went and peered into the box in the airing cupboard. There the Tiny Twins lay, eyes tight shut, paws firmly tucked under, obviously going nowhere.

"They're in here," James told them. "They're not coming out to play."

"I'll bet it's those last two," smiled Mum. "Late to be born and late ever since."

"Like someone else I could mention," grinned Jenny.

They all looked at James.

But James didn't even notice. He was kneeling beside the box watching the twin kittens. And even as he looked he saw a tiny, glinting eye open just a slit. It looked straight at James as if it knew him already – and winked at him! James was delighted, though he couldn't tell which of the Tiny Twins had winked at him.

Whoever it was, he thought, I'm sure it'll know me next time.

Chapter 6

From then on, James felt especially responsible for the Tiny Twins. Of course, he was mad about all of the kittens, but it seemed to him that these two needed a lot of special attention. First thing in the morning, last thing at night, and almost every time he came into the kitchen, he slipped across to the airing cupboard to look at the two smallest kittens.

It wasn't hard to pick them out because the others were soon on the move, rolling around their box and, later, right out of it, skittering about the slippery tiles like furry, fairy skaters. They never got far: Breakfast watched their every move and soon scooted them back into the cupboard when she thought they'd been out long enough.

But the Tiny Twins never even left the cupboard. They stretched themselves out in the unaccustomed space and lay, like a couple of spoons, rolling over only when James tickled their tummies.

"You spend more time on the floor than you do on your feet these days," Dad teased him. "Those last kittens will never get out of the box if you entertain them all the time."

"They're waiting to grow," said James. "They'll come out when they're ready."

Jenny didn't lie on the floor with the kittens – she sat on one of the worktops, cuddling and playing with them.

"As if they were teddy bears or something," James complained.

"Oh no, they're much too lively for teddy bears. Just look at this ginger one!" Jenny laughed as the ginger kitten tried to clamber up into her hair. "He's going to be a big, bad, bold one when he grows up."

"He's going to fall off if you don't watch out," James warned her, as the big, bad, bold kitten made a dash to the edge of the worktop.

"Come here, Ginger," laughed Jenny. "You'd think he was older than all the others, wouldn't you? He's so adventurous."

"Not like the twins," said James, picking one of the smallest kittens out of the box. "You're not ready for adventures yet, are you, Tiny Twin?"

"What did you say?" asked Jenny, sharply. "You know we're not supposed to give them names."

"You did," James reminded her. "You just called that big one Ginger."

Now it was Jenny's turn to blush. "That's not a name, it's a description," she snapped.

"So's Tiny Twin," grinned James. "It describes its size and its relationship to the other Twin."

"Yes, but Carol will want to call them something else," Jenny pointed out. "All the new owners will want to choose a name for their kitten."

"Which owners?" asked James. "We've only found one."

Jenny shrugged. "I expect people will come to see them as soon as the word gets round."

James leant over the box and gently tickled a kitten's ear. He couldn't bear to think of anyone taking the little creatures away.

"Don't get too big and bold," he whispered. "Then perhaps nobody will want to take you away."

The Twins rolled over and peered anxiously up at him. They didn't seem to want to go anywhere, either. For a moment all was peaceful in the utility room. Four of the kittens were enjoying clambering all over Jenny while James sat by the box smoothing the Twins' fluffy greyish fur.

"Come on, you two – supper!" called Mum. "Don't forget to wash your hands and—"

"Shut that door!" chorused the children.

Shut that door had become the family motto – they were always reminding each other about keeping the kittens safely shut in the utility room.

"Easy to lose, hard to find," said Dad. "They can get into places you'd never dream of."

"I bet Breakfast would always find them," said James.

"Probably," Mum agreed. "But as they get older she'll leave them to fend for themselves, you know, and that's when they start getting into trouble."

And that's just what Ginger did.

He'd always been the strongest, boldest – and daftest – of the kittens. He was the first to scramble out of the cupboard, where he immediately fell into Breakfast's drinking water! He sat in the bowl, letting out tiny squawks until Breakfast herself rescued him, wiped him dry, and batted him on the ear. Later on, he was the first to venture out to the kitchen. Nobody noticed the gingery-brown animal slithering about on the gingery-brown tiles, until Mum started pulling at her skirt.

"What's the matter with it?" she muttered. "Something's caught in my skirt!"

She shook her skirt and tried to brush the something off. Only it wasn't a something, and it wouldn't budge!

"Hey, stop!" cried Jenny, almost hysterical with laughter. "There's a ginger kitten climbing up your skirt!"

"Get him off!" cried Mum. "This is my best skirt!"

Jenny knelt behind Mum and tried to dislodge the kitten's strong little claws from the soft, delicate fabric.

"Don't pull," warned Mum. "I don't want it torn."

"I've got the kitten," Jenny explained, "but I can't get his claws out."

"James!" called Mum. "Come in here and help your sister rescue me from this monster!"

James came running in from the utility room where he'd been "chatting" to his twins. He took the tiny paws in his hand and carefully unhooked them, one by one, until it was freed.

"There you are, Mum," said Jenny, taking up the kitten and holding it close. "Skirt and kitten both fine – you can hardly tell where he's been, can you, James?"

James held out the fold of Mum's skirt and looked doubtful. He was sure he could see holes made by the kitten's claws. Jenny nudged him with her foot.

"Oh, no – there's no damage," he assured Mum.

"I told you it'd be hectic once those kittens got on the move," Mum said, rather crossly. "For heaven's sake keep the utility room door shut or they'll get trodden underfoot."

So, after Ginger's Great Escape, every time anyone went into the utility room the cry went up to "Shut that door!" But, one evening, somebody must have forgotten.

"One, two, three, four, five..." said Jenny, counting the kittens into the box at bedtime. "Oh – and where's Ginger?"

"Isn't he in there already?" asked James.

"No. Maybe he's got stuck between the box and the back of the cupboard – hang on..." Jenny leaned in and peered down the back. "No, he's not here."

"I'll check all the corners and the machines," said James. He crawled the length and breadth of the little room, calling, "Here, kitty, kitty! Ginger, come on – supper time!" But there was no answering squeak, no miniature miaow, nothing.

"It's no use," said James anxiously. "I don't think he's even in here."

Jenny stared all round. "Well, where can he be?"

"He was wandering around the kitchen only the other day," James reminded her. "He could be anywhere in the house."

"Or out of it," added Jenny. "Mum's been in the garden all evening and she left the back door open."

"Oh, no!" James's eyes widened in horror. "What if—"

"What if we get on and try to find him," interrupted Jenny. "Kitchen first."

They crept across the kitchen floor, checking every tile, every surface, every corner, every cranny – and still no ginger kitten.

"What on earth are you two playing at?" laughed Dad when he found them on their hands and knees by the cooker.

"Detectives," Jenny grunted. "The Case of the Missing Feline."

"We're looking for the ginger kitten, Dad," James explained. "He's disappeared."

"Oh, no!" groaned Dad. "I warned you – easy to lose, hard to find."

"Impossible, I'd say," Jenny stood up. "We've covered every centimetre of this floor and there's no sign of him."

"Are you sure you've checked the utility room?"

"Every corner," said Jenny.

"Even the washing-machine and the tumble-drier," added James. He sniffed, dismally.

"Why didn't you keep the door closed?" Dad asked irritably.

"We did," they assured him.

"If that's true then he can't be in the kitchen," he pointed out. "Let's go and check the utility room again."

By now the other kittens were tucked up and suckling heartily. Breakfast looked anxiously out at them – she knew her naughty kitten hadn't come home. The children took Dad all round the room, showing him how they'd crept and crawled at kitten height and found nothing.

"Well, it seems you're right," said Dad. "There's no sign of him in here." And, as was his habit, he leaned against the sink and gazed out of the window, as if seeking inspiration – or even a lost kitten.

"It's no use looking out there," Jenny pointed out. "Even the bad, bold ginger couldn't have got out through the window – it's shut."

"I'm just trying to think," said Dad, drumming his fingers on the stainless steel draining-board. "Where could the little blighter have got to?" he muttered, absent-mindedly twisting his fingers around the taps. The children stood watching him hopefully. Maybe Dad would have a wonderful inspiration...

But he didn't – he almost had a disaster. Thinking hard and fiddling with the taps he suddenly fiddled too far and a jet of cold water sprayed down into the sink. Swoosh!

"Wrrrrow!" The ginger kitten leapt out of the sink and on to the worktop, splattering water all over Dad.

"What the—?" Startled, Dad jumped back, shaking drops off his cardigan all over the floor.

"It's Ginger!" cried James, almost crying with relief. "Turn off the tap, Dad! He's frightened!"

"He's not the only one!" said Dad. "I

thought he was the ghost of the plug-hole come to haunt me!" He leaned over and turned the tap off.

But the move frightened Ginger even more and he made a sudden dive off the worktop down to the floor.

"Catch him!" shrieked Jenny.

And James did reach out with open hands and catch the little kitten just as he dropped through the air.

"Well caught, James!" called Jenny, as if they were playing rounders on the beach.

"Oh, you poor, poor kitty," murmured James, holding the shivering, howling kitten close. "Did that water frighten you then?"

"That kitten certainly frightened me," muttered Dad. "How on earth did he get into the sink?"

James looked at Jenny accusingly. They both knew she took the kittens up on to the worktops to play, and now the ginger one had decided he liked it up there.

"He must have climbed up the hand towel." Jenny pointed to the towel which hung from a peg at the end of the sink.

"Just like he climbed up Mum's skirt," smiled Dad.

"And then he fell into the sink," continued James.

"Just like he fell into the water bowl last week," smiled Jenny.

"Well, he must be hungry after his adventure," said James. "I'll put him back in the box. Breakfast will dry him off and feed him."

"I wish somebody would dry me off and

feed me," said Dad, standing dripping all over the floor.

"Poor Dad!" laughed James. "Come on, I'll help you." He reached for the towel and began to pat Dad's dripping trousers.

"I'll make a start on supper," said Jenny, moving off to the kitchen. "And when you've finished in here—"

"Don't forget to shut the door!" chorused Dad and James.

And of course, they didn't – not that time.

Chapter 7

The kittens were really on the move now, and growing fast. They had their own litter box, which needed clearing every day. They were starting to eat special kitten food and to drink water, as Breakfast spent more and more time down the garden and left the kittens to their own devices – and their own food.

"She's weaning them," Dad explained.

"What's that?" asked James.

"Getting them used to solid food for when they go to their new homes."

James felt a lump in his throat – he hated the thought of losing the kittens. Country life was quite bearable while he had them to tend, but once they'd gone he'd have no friends nearby at all. Mum had said he could invite a school friend over at weekends, once they'd really settled in, but "not just yet". And it was no use looking to Jenny for company now – she was totally absorbed in Rosie and her horses. At half-term, Jenny was going to spend her mornings at the stables with Rosie, taking a riding course.

"Will you come and watch?" she asked James.

"I'll be too busy looking after the kittens," he replied.

Jenny looked doubtful. "Mum's working some mornings," she pointed out. "She won't let you stay here all on your own."

"I won't be on my own," said James. "I'll be with seven cats."

"Cats aren't babysitters."

"I don't need a babysitter," James said, indignantly. "I *am* the babysitter – for the kittens."

Jenny shrugged. "Mum will never agree."

And she was right.

"No, James," said his mother. "You'll have

to go with Dad to the workshop at least for the first two mornings – I can't get off until Wednesday."

"But I was going to look after the kittens," he protested.

"Breakfast will do that perfectly well without you. After all, she's managed the first few weeks on her own while you've been at school."

"Yes, but they're growing now. They need exercise and entertainment."

"So what are you going to do with them?" grinned Jenny. "Take them jogging then sit them in front of the television?"

"No, silly, I've thought up lots of little games for them—"

"Like hide and seek in the sink?"

James scowled. "It's all right for you," he said. "You're going off to play with horses all day while all I've got to do is hang around Dad's workshop."

"It's only for a couple of mornings," said Mum. "And you love the place, you know you do."

That much was true, though James was in

no mood to admit it. He loved pottering about amongst the wood and the shavings, making a little something out of nothing – a fat, round owl, with shavings for feathers, a tiny dragon with prickles down his back...

James closed his eyes for a moment, feeling a chunk of wood smooth between his fingers, smelling the pungent scent of it as he rubbed it into shape. He hadn't been to the Old Mill since the family had moved out of town – it would be almost like a half-term treat. He opened his eyes again and saw that his mother was watching him closely.

"You could make some little toys for the kittens," she suggested.

James's face brightened. "I could invent something that would give them exercise and entertainment," he said thoughtfully.

"Oh, that's easy-peasy!" said Jenny. "Bring them back a bag of mice – there's lots of them at the mill!"

"Ugh! And you'd better leave them there," said Mum. "Dad's idea is to take a kitten to catch the mice, not bring the mice to the kitten!"

James frowned; more and more he was beginning to hate the idea of the kittens going to work at the mill. Still, he told himself, on Monday he'd be able to check up to see whether it would make a decent home for a cat.

So on Monday morning they shut Breakfast and the kittens into the utility room and dropped Jenny off at the stables.

"We'll pick you up at lunchtime," Mum told her. "Pay attention to all the instructors and take care!"

But Jenny had just caught sight of Rosie

and she dashed across without even pausing to wave goodbye.

"Rosie!" they heard her calling. "Are you riding with me?"

Rosie shook her head and James saw her turn to a gloomy-looking boy who was standing with her. As the car pulled away James glanced back and saw Jenny and Rosie deep in conversation together, quite ignoring the boy beside them, who stared straight ahead, glum and silent.

I wonder what he's doing there? thought James. Well, he must like riding or he wouldn't be at the stables. Still, he certainly didn't look very happy at the prospect of a morning with the horses – and the girls!

James suddenly smiled – his morning might prove more interesting than Jenny's, after all. He sat back and spent the rest of the journey into town thinking about his Great Invention.

"Bye, James!" said Mum, as she dropped him off on her way to the office. "I'll try to get away promptly, all right?"

"Right." James nodded, hoping she wouldn't be too prompt. His Great Plan would take quite a time.

"I'll set you up with a workbench and some tools," said Dad once they were in the mill. "But you must keep to your own work space – don't go wandering near the big machines."

"Can I have some wood?" asked James.

Dad nodded. "I'll leave you a stack of off-cuts," he said. "Now, I'm going to be busy in the machine shop. If you need anything, just ask Carol."

Carol was a good student – she loved wood. At Christmas she'd given Jenny a beautifully carved jewel box and James a game of solitaire – a wooden plate with 45 dimples and 45 polished wooden balls to fit into them. James had played with it more than any of his Christmas toys. It wasn't only an interesting game, it was beautiful to touch and smell and hold. Maybe she'd like to help him with his Great Plan? James wondered. After all, if she was taking charge of the mill kittens, she'd be interested in their training.

But Carol had no time to spare just then.

"I've got to finish off a chair this morning," she told him. "What are you going to do?"

"I'm going to make some equipment for our kittens," he said.

"That's a great idea," said Carol. "They must be ready to play around by now. When are we getting our two?"

"Oh, they can't leave home for weeks yet," James told her. "But they've got their eyes open and their coats are growing. You can tell which is which now, except for the Tiny Twins."

"Twins?" asked Carol. "Surely they're all twins – I mean, born at the same time?"

James explained about the two kittens being born together.

"Sounds as if they'd be just right for here," Carol said. "Your dad says I can choose which ones we're having."

James's face dropped. He looked around at the vast, high space of the workshop, listened to the tooth-splitting screech of the electric cutters in the next room, and thought about his beloved little kittens.

Carol was watching him.

"I thought I'd keep them in my place until they're older."

"Your place?" asked James.

Carol nodded. "You know – the flats above here." She pointed up to the great beams in the ceiling. "They only just finished the building work a couple of weeks ago. I'm still sort of camping out up there. Would you like to see?"

James followed Carol out of the workshop and up the stone steps which ran along the end wall outside the mill. He paused at the top of the stone staircase while Carol unlocked a heavy wooden door.

"Here we are!" She flung it open and stood back. "In you go!"

James stepped into a low, surprisingly light room. Surprising because the windows were small and deep, ranged at the far end, and the walls were raw brick. He looked up and saw that the brilliant light came from four flat windows set into the roof either side of the great central beam. He could see clouds scudding across them, as if they were films on television. And two tall, narrow windows were set deep in the end wall, like slits of sunshine.

"Oh, it's lovely!" he cried.

"Yes, it is," agreed Carol. "Be even better when I can afford some furniture." And she indicated a rough plank table, supported on four piles of bricks, and a mattress under the window, where she obviously slept.

"Luckily, the kitchen and bathroom are fully equipped," she said. "At least I can eat and wash." She looked at James's wondering face. "Do you think your kittens would like it here?" she asked.

James swallowed hard. "It's a bit empty," he admitted. "If you had a basket or a box..."

Carol nodded. "Of course," she said. "I've got a box but it's full of my tools at the moment. Talking of which..." she looked at her watch, "we must be getting along or your dad'll be wondering when that chair is going to be finished."

Back in the workshop, James sorted out bits of off-cuts and laid them on the workbench. There were some pieces of dowelling and a couple of thicker chunks which Carol had discarded when she was making the chair legs. The rest were flat pieces of plywood, in a variety of shapes and sizes, and a square chunk of chipboard. James stared at them for a moment, then, picking up one of the leg pieces, he began to fit things together.

It was no use being too ambitious, he knew; neither Carol nor his dad would have time to help. But he was used to woodworking – he'd helped Dad at home for many years now and was quite safe with his own junior-sized tools. He picked up a strip of wood and measured it along one side of the chipboard.

"Yes!" he said to himself. "There's enough for each side..."

He carefully marked out the lengths and cut them off with his hacksaw and gradually built up a kind of frame which ran along the sides of the chipboard.

"Like the bird table back at the old house," he reminded himself. He'd made a bird table for the garden when he was younger. Well, Dad had been around then to help with the tricky bits, but now he was sure he could manage it again all on his own – though what he was making wasn't anything so simple as a bird table...

He was so absorbed in his work that he didn't so much as lift up his head until he heard Mum's voice as she greeted Carol.

"Come on, James – it's lunchtime already and we've got to pick up Jenny from the stables."

James looked up rather vaguely.

"Oh," he said. "Is that the time?"

"It's past that time," said Mum, crisply. "Do get a move on."

"Can't I stay here and finish this?" he asked, peering at the neatly framed "tabletop".

Mum laughed and looked across at Carol. "And this is the boy who sulked for hours about having to come to the workshop!" she said. "Sorry, love, but Dad's working late tonight so you'd better come with me." She turned to go. "Right now, please!" she added, as James picked up another wooden shape.

"Put all your bits in here," said Carol, handing him a box. "You can finish it off tomorrow."

"Good idea," said Mum. "It'll give you something to look forward to while Jenny's off riding. How's the flat coming along, Carol?"

Carol grimaced. "Ask James – he's been up to inspect it." She turned to James. "Bye, James! Give the kittens a hug from me."

James smiled in a dazed kind of way, followed his mother out and clambered into the back of the car. He hadn't even thought about the kittens for the past couple of hours, he realized, even though he'd been making the toy for them. Not a toy – a piece of equipment, he corrected himself. He clicked his safety belt and sat back, brooding on the next phase of his work.

Jenny was nowhere to be seen when they arrived at the stables. Mum went off to find her while James sat in a dream, looking vacantly out of the open window. He was watching some amazingly small children leading their very small ponies round and round the paddock when someone caught his eye: a solitary figure, sitting on top of the fence, staring gloomily out into space.

It was the boy who'd been with Rosie earlier. James wondered why he'd come to the stables at all – he obviously wasn't enjoying being there. He watched the hunched-up figure, looking just like he'd so often felt when Rosie and Jenny went off together. Somebody else with nothing to do in the holidays, he thought. And then he smiled – well, he'd got plenty to do now he had his Great Invention.

Chapter 8

As soon as he got home, James went off to kitten-watch. He'd have to look more closely now he'd started on the Great Invention. As they pranced about the place, and rolled and rollicked, he was mentally measuring them up – the length of their legs, the stretch of their backs, the reach of their heads. He'd need to know all this if his plan was to work. He was so preoccupied with his Great Invention that he didn't notice Jenny's changed mood until next day.

"You gone off horses?" James enquired as they drove an unusually silent Jenny to her riding course next morning.

"I've gone off small boys," she said, glaring at him.

James merely grinned at her. Nothing could upset him just then. He was planning to assemble his Great Invention that morning and bring it home for the kittens.

"I didn't know you knew any small boys," he said mildly.

"I know one who's hanging around making life a misery for Rosie and me," she said.

"Oh, the gloomy lad," said James.

"He's gloomy all right – he's a right pain." Jenny sighed heavily. "Rosie's got to look after him all week and he won't go near a horse."

"I don't blame him," said James, with feeling.

"Well, if you're so sympathetic why don't you look after him?" replied Jenny, sharply.

"No way! I'm too busy."

"Busy playing with the kittens, I suppose," said Jenny, scornfully.

"Better than playing with horses."

"We don't *play* with horses."

"Yes, you do."

"No, we don't."

"You do."

"We don't."

"Do."

"Don't."

"Hey, you two, stop squabbling in the back there!" said Dad. "I can't hear myself think."

Jenny sniffed and turned to glare out of her window. James smiled quietly to himself and worked out how to fix his dowelling more firmly.

"Why don't you ask them over?" Mum suggested. "The boy can come back with me tomorrow morning and Rosie can come to lunch. It might cheer the boy up a bit."

Jenny pulled a face. "Invite him?" she asked scornfully. "He'll only mope and mooch around. He hates the country, he hates animals – what can we do with him?"

"Oh, James will think of something, won't you, love?"

James stared so hard at his mother's back he almost expected her to feel a stab of pain.

"You can show him the kittens," she went on, oblivious of his look.

"Yeah, you do that, James. Rosie and I can go down the field to her horses," said Jenny, brightening up. "Great! I'll ask them. Thanks, Mum!" Jenny scrambled out of the car and she ran across the stable yard, waving excitedly to Rosie and the gloomy boy at her side.

And now it was James's turn to feel gloomy. All he wanted to do tomorrow was to test out his Great Invention on the kittens, and he didn't want any witnesses. He realized it wasn't perfect, it would need a bit of adjusting here and there, and the kittens might need a little time to get used to it. But that was what the rest of the holiday was for, so far as James was concerned. Not for entertaining gloomy little boys.

But as soon as he got down to work James cheered up. If that dratted gloomy boy didn't like the countryside and animals, he could just push off and play on the computer, or sit in front of the TV all day – anything so long as he didn't get in the way of the Great Invention. He bent over the workbench and screwed a small hook into the side of the board so hard that it almost split the wood.

"Steady on!" he told himself. "Don't spoil everything now, just because Old Gloomy Face is coming round!"

But he soon forgot the prospect of Old Gloomy Face as he shaped and sanded and waxed and polished, until all the bits of the Great Invention were (almost) perfect. James set them out on the bench and frowned.

"Hey, they look great!" said Carol, passing on her way to the machine shop. "You've got the gift, James."

"Gift?" he asked, puzzled. Nobody had offered him a present.

"You know – like your father." She stopped and leaned on the bench for a moment. "It's not everybody who can work wood," she said seriously. "I mean, lots of people can assemble pieces – kitchen units, shelves, the usual stuff – but here we're all craftsmen and women, with a feeling for wood – a gift if you like." She stood up. "And I think you've got it – straight from your dad, I suppose."

"And my grandad," said James.

"Ah, must be in the genes."

"Not in Jenny's," James grinned. "Mum says she's cack-handed."

"Well, everybody's different, you know, even in the same family." Carol smiled and went on into the machine shop.

"What?" James was suddenly struck by a brilliant idea: if he watched the kittens carefully when they tried out his Great Invention, he'd see how different each little character was. Or, in the case of the twins, how much the same – he was sure they'd both do exactly the same thing. He smiled as he picked up his bits and pieces. He couldn't wait to show Miss Clever Clogs that he hadn't been mistaken about the twins.

But Jenny was nowhere to be seen when they called for her at the stables.

"I'm going to the office to book her weekend lesson," said Mum. "You go and look for her."

James wandered over to the paddock and leaned over the gate, then backed off hastily as several ponies shoved their heavy noses into his chest, nuzzling at his sweatshirt.

"Hey, get off! I haven't got anything for you!" he exclaimed.

"I don't think they bite," came a voice from the grassy bank, "though I wouldn't actually trust them."

James looked round and saw the gloomy boy, sitting on the branch of a tree that overhung the paddock.

"You come for your sister?" he asked.

James nodded.

"She's in the loose boxes with Rosie," said the boy. "They're crazy on grooming."

"They're crazy on horses," said James.

"They're crazy full stop," said the boy.

They eyed each other up, warily, and then they both laughed.

Suddenly the boy slid down from his tree.

"Rosie says we're coming over to your place tomorrow," he said. "I can't wait. It must be better than this." He gestured around the stables and paddock.

"Well, there's nothing very special about our place," said James, hastily. He didn't want the boy to expect too much.

"Oh, yes, there is – you haven't got horses," grinned the boy.

"No, but we've got six kittens," said James.

He'd meant this as a warning, as Jenny had said Rosie's cousin hated animals. But to his surprise the boy's eyes lit up.

"I'd rather have kittens than horses any day. At least they're small and tame."

"Small, but not very tame," said James. "If you want to play with them you'd better bring your gloves – their teeth are like needles."

"Oh, I expect I'll be happy just watching," the boy said. "I like observing animals. That's what I was doing up there." He nodded towards the tree and suddenly pulled a notebook out of his back pocket.

"Observing the horses?" asked James.

"No, something much more interesting." He flipped the pages over. "I was timing the ants."

"Timing the ants?" Now James really was surprised – and interested. It was the sort of thing he might have done himself had he thought of it.

"Yes, you see every single ant has a specific job to do, so I thought I'd follow one ant on his morning's work – sort of time-and-motion study, you know?"

Fascinated, James nodded.

"Only thing is," said the boy, "I've no way of marking my ant and I kept losing him and picking on another." He snapped the notebook shut. "Another unsuccessful experiment!"

"But interesting," said James, politely. He paused, wondering whether to take the boy into his confidence about the Great Invention. After all, that was a kind of time-and-motion study. But before he could begin to explain he heard his mother calling.

"James! Jenny's here now. Come on!"

"See you tomorrow then," said the boy, raising a hand in a salute.

"Tomorrow," said James. "See you!"

As he ran across to the car he suddenly realized he didn't even know the gloomy boy's name. If he was coming to visit he could hardly go on referring to him as "the gloomy boy".

"What's he called then?" he asked his sister.

"Who?"

"Rosie's gloomy friend."

"Oh, you mean Ben – Ben Bowers. He's not a friend, he's her cousin."

"And he's not really gloomy," added James. "At least he wasn't when I was talking to him."

"Well, there you are," said Mum. "You've cheered him up already."

It was James who needed cheering up that evening as he tried to set up his Great

Invention for the thirty-first time. It had been all right back at the workshop, fitting a bit here, adjusting a screw there, but once he got it back home all the pieces seemed to have grown and nothing fitted quite right. James struggled with his hammer and screwdriver, pushing the centre pole up through the hole in the tabletop, tightening the supporting legs at the bottom, but no matter what adjustments he made, the whole edifice wobbled.

His idea had been to make a kind of miniature bird table, supported by a scratching pole, with various toys dangling from its ledges so that the kittens could play with the toys, sharpen their claws (as if they needed to!) and, if they were bold enough, clamber up the post and out on to the "table" at the top, where they would find a "mouse" to pounce on, which was really a hollow bit of wood with some cheese inside.

And now, after talking to Ben, he'd thought of something else he could do while the kittens played on the apparatus. He could observe them, make notes, time them...

The trouble was, as soon as he started to erect the apparatus, the kittens came out to play. Amused at first, James allowed them to scramble and tumble around, as he pushed and pressed and hammered the pieces together. But the kittens were excited, ready to pounce on anything and everything. Each time James managed to get a piece to fit, they managed to pull it apart again!

Eventually he had to move it on to the worktop and after a while it was all ready and (almost) erect. Cautiously (for it was still rather wobbly) James put it down on the floor and joggled the dangling strings so that a little bell jingled, a ping-pong ball bounced, a string of big wooden beads rattled ... and the kittens came tumbling out, fast and curious, to investigate the noise.

Big Ginger was first, naturally, and of course he made for the centre pole. He sniffed the thick layer of sacking that James had wrapped round it as a claw-sharpener. But Ginger wasn't at all interested in sharpening his claws – he wanted to climb the pole. He jumped up on his hind legs and stretched out his front paws, digging his claws into the sacking to get a good hold.

"Well done, Ginger!" said Jenny, who, of course, arrived just in time for the opening ceremony.

"He's more intelligent than we thought," said James, with satisfaction.

"And heavier," Jenny pointed out as the pole keeled over. Ginger clung on, squawking loudly, as the whole edifice collapsed among a heap of other kittens, who had the sense to scuttle back to their nice, safe cupboard, howling for their mother.

Jenny, too, collapsed – with laughter – while James bent to extricate Big Ginger from the tattered sacking.

"Oh, I see, it's a kitten-scarer," said Jenny, when she'd recovered. "Useful for keeping them off Mum's garden."

"It'll be all right when I've glued it." Almost in tears, James turned his back firmly towards the door and bent to pick up the scattered pieces.

"You could ask Ben to help tomorrow," said Jenny, a little more kindly. "Rosie calls him the Mad Professor – he's always making inventions."

"What sort of inventions?" James laid out the remains of his own Great Invention on the worktop and set to untangling the strings.

Jenny shrugged. "I don't know," she admitted. "But Rosie says he designs things on his computer and then makes models."

James grunted. "This isn't a model," he said. "It's educational equipment."

"Yeah?" Jenny grinned. "Well, I suppose it might teach them to keep away from bird tables when they get older." She backed out of the utility room hastily.

"Ask Ben!" she called again, on her way upstairs.

Chapter 9

Ben, it turned out, was quite an expert. As soon as he arrived he took one look at the sad disarray of James's equipment and asked for coarse sandpaper. He spread all the pieces on the worktop and he set to, rubbing and scraping, smoothing every part which connected to another.

"You see," he said, solemnly, "when you fit the bits together they need coaxing, not forcing."

"Like horses?" grinned James.

Ben gave him a baleful look.

"More use," he said, picking up the centre pole and rubbing it hard.

They were sitting on the floor of the utility

room, smothered in tiny kittens. Ben ignored them, merely brushing them aside when they got between him and his work, but James hovered between kittens and woodwork, worrying about both.

"You have to be especially careful with the Tiny Twins," he said, as he plucked the two smallest kittens off Ben's sweater. "They're very delicate."

"Twins?" Ben queried. "But they're all from the same litter – they must be sextuplets."

"Yes, but these last two were born together – they're identical. Even the white splodges are in the same shape and in the same place..." James turned them on their backs and tried to show Ben how their fur was taking on identical patterns. "And look at their little noses – they've even got the same black freckles."

"Yes, but have they got the same number of freckles?" Ben spoke without even turning round to look at the twin kittens.

For a moment James almost started to count them, then he laughed. "Does everything have to be absolutely accurate for you?" he asked.

"No, I'm just interested. If you're right, and two were born together, that's a scientific phenomenon."

"A what?"

"A unique natural event." Ben bent over his work and rubbed more vigorously. "All the kittens belong to a single litter, but each one is individually marked. Identical animals are usually bred from pedigree stock. So how come these two kittens are identical? Something in their genes, I suppose..."

By now Ben wasn't really speaking to James, just musing to himself. James was still listening though, fascinated to hear his own thoughts spoken. He, too, had pondered this phenomenon, though never aloud.

For a moment neither of them spoke; the silence was broken only by the steady rasping of sandpaper on wood and the various high-pitched squeaks of the kittens. Suddenly James became aware of a deeper, purring sound and when he looked round he saw that Breakfast was back from her outing in the garden. Then, just as if she'd called them, the kittens rolled off Ben's lap, scrambled down James's sweatshirt and trotted across the floor to their mother.

"Isn't it amazing how they go off to meet their mum like that?" said James.

"Going to meet their breakfast, more like."

James groaned. "We've had that joke from Dad every morning since the kittens were born," he said. "And anyway, they had their breakfast hours ago."

Even so, the kittens followed Breakfast back into the cupboard, and rummaged about in her deep fur for their mid-morning snack.

Now Ben turned to watch. "There you are!" he said triumphantly. "Instinct." And he went on with his work in silence.

James suddenly felt rather shy – and rather redundant. The kittens were either feeding or sleeping, safe in their box, and Ben was obviously getting on very well without his help. There was really nothing for him to do. James shuffled himself on to the worktop and fiddled nervously with the taps. Then, remembering Dad's accident, he stopped, gazed out of the window and hummed softly to himself, wishing he could think of something to say to Ben.

As if he'd read his mind, Ben suddenly spoke.

"We ought to try to set this up while they're all out of the way."

"The kittens or the girls?" asked James.

"Both," said Ben, shortly. "Can you help me to get this bit in nice and tightly?"

James shuffled over and showed Ben how the pieces were meant to fit. They worked together in silence, and when they had finished they stood back. The Great Invention looked quite impressive now, with the main post standing firmly in the base, arches and tunnels placed carefully on the platform, leading to a little cage at the side, where James planned to hide the "treasure" for the hunter.

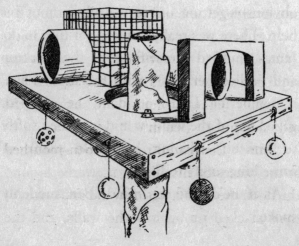

"Ingenious," murmured Ben. "Like one of those mazes for testing the intelligence of rats."

"Yes, well, that's the sort of thing I was after," said James eagerly. "I didn't want just a toy, but something more ... er ... stimulating."

"Could be stupefying if it collapses on them again," smiled Ben. "Got any glue?"

"Only about twenty different kinds. Come and choose."

James led the way across the yard to the old outhouse.

"Where are you two off to?" called Mum from the terrace, where she was hauling great stones around to build up a rockery.

"Just borrowing a bit of glue," said James.

"Make sure you put it back in exactly the right place so that Dad can find it again."

"I will," James promised. He heaved at the old door and let Ben in.

"Wow!" Ben gazed round, open-mouthed at the pieces of machinery scattered around the floor, the neat layers of wood and boxes of tools stacked up against the walls, and the rows of paint pots, varnish tins, bottles of wood-stain, and the huge tubes of glue, standing on a couple of workbenches. "It's like Aladdin's cave!"

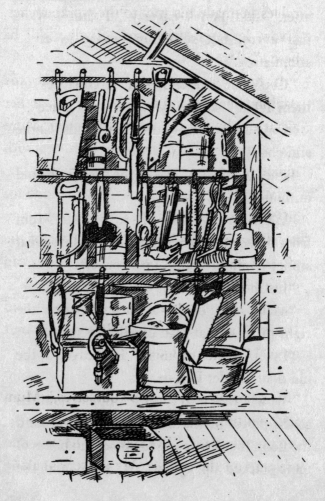

"Without the jewels," said James. "Though I expect Dad'll produce a few – this is going to be his studio for special hand-crafted work." Stepping over a mound of cables he made his way to the workbenches. "Now, let's see, what sort of glue will be best..."

It took quite a long time to take the equipment apart and glue each joint together again and by the time they'd finished, Mum was already calling them to help her with lunch.

"We'd better leave the apparatus alone for an hour or so," said Ben, "just to make sure it's all quite stable." He cleaned the top of the glue off with some tissue and screwed the cap on firmly.

"I'll take this back to the garage," said James. "You go into the kitchen – and don't forget to shut the door..."

"It's picnic lunch, so help yourselves," Mum said, putting out bowls of tuna mayonnaise, crisps and salads. "I've fixed the big wooden table up on the terrace. My rockery's taking

shape now – the planting's looking good..."
She paused for a moment and gazed through
the kitchen window at her new garden.
Recognizing the signs of a creative mind at
work, James took a couple of tuna rolls for
starters, poured lemonade into plastic
beakers and he and Ben took their lunch
outside.

Ignoring the newly-erected wooden table,
the two boys sat on the old stone wall at the
edge of the terrace, chewing tuna baps,
slurping cloudy lemonade and talking,
talking, talking. James hadn't talked to
anyone like this for months. He told Ben all
about the house move, the arrival of
Breakfast, and, later, the kittens.

"I only hope our move is as interesting," said Ben, looking suddenly gloomy again.

"Your move?"

"Yeah." Ben chewed silently for a few moments, as if making up his mind whether to elaborate. "We've got to move up here for Mum's job."

"What about your dad's job?"

"Oh, he works all over the place," said Ben. "He's an engineer. So long as we're near an airport he doesn't mind where we live."

"Like round here?" James tried not to sound too eager.

Ben sat still for a moment, looking across the valley where cloud shadows scudded across the dark moorland and down through the forest below. It was so quiet on the terrace now, he could even hear the rattle of the stream half a mile below. He sighed and swivelled round to face the house, his back to the valley.

"I never wanted to move up here," he admitted. "That's why I came to stay with my cousin Rosie – to see if I liked it." He grinned at James. "Another failed experiment."

"Why?"

"Well, look at it!" Ben gestured. "All these fields, the woods, those hills – I mean, what do you do in your spare time?"

"What do *you* do?" asked James, dodging the question.

"Work on the computer, mainly."

He'd said work not play, James noted. Ben seemed a bit like himself – not one for playing around.

"You can do that here," he pointed out.

"I suppose so," Ben agreed. "But then, what about other things – shops, cinema, library, swimming..."

James shrugged. "Library and swimming pool are at school – that's only a bus- or bike-ride away and we're there all week anyhow. I go to the library one evening and swimming club another."

"So what do you do at the weekends?"

"Well..." James suddenly realized he did very little. "I've been a bit busy with the kittens since we came here."

Ben sat up. "Hey, that reminds me – let's go and see how they're getting on with the apparatus."

They collected the plates and debris and walked back up to the house together. James suddenly felt really happy, as if it were Christmas or something. There was a chance that Ben might move into the area, come to their school, even be his best friend...

But as soon as they got into the kitchen James's happiness drained away.

"What's that?" asked Ben, standing in the middle of the kitchen, listening to the strange cacophony of sounds like distant sea-gulls, or a baby crying...

"It's the kittens!" James shot across the floor and flung open the door.

The first thing he saw was Breakfast, running around nudging and licking at several kittens who were scrambling about the floor, squeaking and squealing, and apparently unable to get up on their legs. Breakfast made a sudden dive, picked up a tabby in her mouth and shot off outside.

"Quick – shut the door!" James issued the standard family order.

"No!" said Ben. "Leave it open! Can't you see what's happened?"

"Yes, Breakfast's moving them out."

"She's doing the right thing – instinct again, I suppose."

"But they'll get lost out there..."

"And they'll get very sick in here – smell!"

James gave a great sniff – and then realized.

"It's fumes from the glue!" he said. "That's why they're all—"

"Drunk?" grinned Ben. "I think we'd better get them all out of here and leave the door open for a while."

They picked up the floppy little animals and rushed them into the kitchen, where James's mum was hunting through a drawer.

"Have you seen the car keys, James?" she asked, looking up.

"You've left the boot open as usual. I bet the keys are still in the lock," said James, breathlessly. "We're moving the kittens out, Mum – state of emergency!"

She looked up then, and saw what the boys were carrying. "What on earth's going on?" she demanded. "I saw Breakfast running out a moment ago and I could have sworn she had a kitten in her mouth."

"She had," said James, and he started to explain, holding up a kitten to demonstrate. And suddenly it all seemed very funny. Both he and Ben fell about laughing, leaning against the kitchen table and clutching hold of their sleepy kittens.

Mum took a hard look at them then went across to the utility room and flung open the end window. Then she picked up the Great Invention and strode off with it.

"And you'd better bring the rest of those kittens out here," she called. "You could all do with some fresh air."

Breakfast was there, on the terrace, anxiously waiting for the rest of her brood. Mum dropped the apparatus down on the table. And it didn't break, noted James, with interest. Not a single piece shifted.

"Glue fumes!" said Mum. "You should have known better, James, after all these years of helping Dad."

"I do!" protested James. "But I'm so used to keeping that door shut, I never thought about the fumes."

"... and the sun streaming in and the boiler on – it was like an oven in there," Mum went on.

"Still, they're reviving now," said Ben.

They all looked towards Breakfast, who was rounding up her kittens. They were obviously excited to find themselves out of doors, and in no hurry to go back to Mummy. They rolled over and over on the flagstones, chased petals and leaves, prowled around the plant pots as if tracking something down, pounced on their own shadows and on each other...

"I must get my camera," said Mum. "You keep an eye on them."

It wasn't easy. The more the kittens explored, the more confident they became and the further they wanted to go. The ginger one was first up to the top of the rockery.

"Look at that!" exclaimed Ben. "Big Ginge, lord of all he surveys!"

He was quickly followed by the two tabbies, who swarmed up the rocks more quickly than even Big Ginge himself, but then slithered down the other side, just for fun. The pale, shy kitten, who was now growing thick grey fur like a teddy bear, set off well, but soon stopped to investigate the plants and flowers. And the Tiny Twins, of course, went no further than the first rock, sat down, snuggled together in the sunshine, and fell asleep.

Luckily, none of them could scale the terrace wall so they were quite safe for the moment. Ben and James had a great time rounding them all up and placing them on strategic rocks to pose for photographs. But just as they got them all, including Breakfast, lined up for a family portrait, the camera gave a whirring sound and a click.

"Oh – that's the end of the film," Mum said. "Never mind. I've got some lovely shots of them at play."

"I'll put another film in for you," Ben offered. "I'm good with cameras."

"I'm sure you are, Ben," smiled Mum, "but it's high time I went to collect the girls from the stables. Now, can I trust you to get these animals back indoors?"

"Of course," said James, quickly. He'd just had an idea about the apparatus. The fumes would have subsided now and it would be interesting to see whether the kittens would want to play on it, given all the distractions out here...

"Right!" Mum glanced across the yard to the car. "Now I must be off – it'll be all right to put the kittens back into the room, now, but don't forget—"

"To shut the door," chorused the boys.

"And the window," added Mum.

"And your boot," added James, indicating the back of the car.

"Oh, yes – it's full of kitty-litter," said Mum. "Could you unload it for me, please, Ben? Leave it by the back door."

So Ben went off to be porter while James was cat-minder, and, finally, Mum went off.

"I suppose we'd better take them back in," said Ben, watching one of the Twins treading delicately between two urns.

"Hang on a minute," said James. "Let's see if they'll go on the apparatus while it's outdoors..."

But the kittens were too distracted to play. As fast as they put one on the apparatus it jumped off to chase a passing butterfly, an insect or even another kitten. Eventually the boys had to give up.

"It's no use," James complained. "They'll never get the hang of it out here."

"Maybe they'll concentrate better indoors," said Ben.

"OK, let's take them in," agreed James. "Three each. I'll take the Twins..."

"And maybe we should leave the apparatus out a while longer," Ben suggested, "just to make sure all the fumes are gone."

James nodded. "The utility room's probably aired off now. We'll tuck them up in the cupboard and leave them to rest for a bit."

"And you said you'd show me your computer," Ben reminded him. "Have you got Doom II?"

"Oh, yes," said James, casually. "I've just beaten the Boss on Level Five."

Ben looked very impressed. "If that's what you have time for when you live in the country," he grinned, "maybe I'll like it after all!"

Chapter 10

The rest of that week, Mum took Jenny to the stables and brought Ben back with her.

"Like changing a library book," she teased. "One sister in, one surrogate brother out."

"Well, at least he's not horse crazy," said James, defensively.

And not cat crazy either, he thought anxiously. If Ben became as bored with kittens as he was with horses, what could they do? It was obvious to James that his rather basic computer wasn't in Ben's league.

"Dad's got an Apple Mac down at the workshop," he explained, once they'd exhausted the limited possibilities of his own computer. "It has some terrific software."

Ben nodded. "Yeah, that's what you need for designing things." He looked at James and grinned. "When I get home I'll draw up some plans for a really tough kitten maze."

"But by the time I've made it they'll be gone," James said, ruefully.

"Have you found homes for them all?"

"Only two so far." James told him about the workshop working kittens.

"Hey, that's great. I think most domestic animals are bored; they need a job to do to keep them alert and healthy."

James felt a sudden surge of relief. He hadn't thought about it like that. If Ben was right, the workshop kittens were in for an exciting life.

Meantime, they were all at home, though not always in the utility room. After that first day in the garden, Breakfast had made it clear that she wanted her kittens to get out and about more, sometimes chasing one or two of them through the door, occasionally carrying a Tiny Twin in her mouth and posting it through the cat flap.

"She's getting them ready to leave home," said Mum. "They'll be quite safe on the terrace, so long as you're keeping an eye on them."

That was much more easily said than done! Forgetting their computer games, the boys spent most of the morning counting kittens. Breakfast was no help at all; she seemed to think she'd done her duty by introducing her brood to the great outdoors – after that, they were on their own. She settled down in a sunny patch on the paving stones and snoozed while her brood skittered about the terrace, chasing anything that moved.

Dancing around on two back legs they chased dandelion seeds; stretching upwards to twice their normal length they batted the heads off potted plants; rolling together in a kind of feline rugby scrum they fought over a flying leaf. James needn't have worried about Ben being bored – he was soon engrossed in his new hobby of kitten-watching, making notes and drawing sketches of the kittens' progress.

"Trouble is, they've got no names," he complained as he sat scribbling at the big wooden table on the terrace.

"We can't give them names," James explained. "They'll only have to learn a new name when they get a new home."

"Well, it's making my notes a mess," Ben declared. "I'll have to give them names in my notebook, but I won't tell them."

James smiled to himself: Ben was taking this kitten-watching very seriously. "What have you called them?" he asked.

"Well..." Ben flicked over a page. "I can't actually tell the difference between the two tabbies and those two black and white ones you say are twins. I've just listed them as Tabby One, Tabby Two and Twin A and B."

"Right. And what about the others?"

"That pale one is Smoky-grey."

"Hey, that's a good name for her!" he said, surprised. He'd never noticed that the palest kitten was now growing a thick grey coat.

"And, of course, there's Big Ginge," Ben went on.

"And that's a great name for him. Just look at him now!" James nodded across the patio, where the ginger kitten stepped silently along the low wall, staring fixedly at something a few metres ahead.

"Like a miniature tiger," Ben said quietly.

Step by step, almost down on his little belly, Big Ginge stalked onwards, and now the boys caught sight of his prey; a yellow butterfly sunning itself on the old stone wall. The kitten padded closer, closer, then crouched, ready to pounce...

Only James pounced first.

"Come down!" he cried, snatching Big Ginge off the wall. "You're not supposed to be up there."

"You've ruined his hunting," Ben protested.

"And saved a butterfly," James pointed out, as the creature fluttered off, oblivious of its narrow escape.

"He was only practising," said Ben. "He's going to be a great hunter when he grows up."

"He won't live to grow up if he falls off the wall," said James. "There's a two-metre drop into the field below."

"He won't fall – not Big Gingc," laughed Ben. "He's a true survivor."

They both had reason to remember those words the next day. It was the hottest day of the holiday – and the last. At the weekend Ben's parents would be coming to collect him and take him back to London. But they'd be back, he assured James: in the summer holidays they'd be house-hunting before moving north. He sounded quite glad about that, James noticed. He hoped they'd move somewhere close, so that Ben could come to his school – and maybe he could use Ben's fabulous computer.

Meantime, Ben was more interested in kittens than computers. They'd all come out to play, but it was so hot that most of them were already nodding off close to Breakfast in the shade of a bush by the old wall. Both boys and kittens were so stupefied that even James began to find kitten-watching a bore.

"Let's take them into the kitchen," suggested Ben. "It'll be cooler there – give us a chance to try out our tests with the apparatus."

"Good idea! You collect that lot with Breakfast and I'll round up the others."

Just as they were carrying the kittens back, Mum pulled into the yard.

"Could you help me unload the boot?" she called. "I've been to the garden centre..."

"And bought half a tonne of stone, no doubt," muttered James. Aloud, he said, "OK, just putting the kittens back in."

It wasn't stones, it was huge bags of compost. By the time Ben and James had wheeled them round to the garden shed, Mum had made a jug of her special fruity cocktail and they all sat in the shade of the big umbrella on the patio. It was so quiet they could hear the waterfall just across the valley.

Ben looked out at the green hillside and sighed. "It's great here," he said. "I never thought I'd like it in the country but I'm really looking forward to coming back."

"It won't always be like this," James's mum warned him. She knew these hills – she'd grown up there. "You should try it in the winter with the everlasting mists and mud."

"And snow," James reminded her. "That'll be fun!"

"Well, yes, but it's no fun in the howling wind and lashing rain. Remember when we first arrived?"

"Oh, I shouldn't mind that," Ben assured her. "James could always come and play on my computer."

Mum raised her eyebrows. "Your parents are moving up here, are they?" she asked.

Ben grinned. "Not yet," he said.

They all looked at each other and laughed.

"I hope they find somewhere as nice as this," said Mum. "There's an old farmhouse over Lowmoor way."

"Where's that?" asked Ben.

James nodded across the valley. "Over there," he said. "Next stop on our school bus."

"That might suit us," said Ben.

"Well, I don't know – it needs a lot doing to it," James's mum warned him.

But Ben wasn't at all put off. "Mum would like that," he said. "She's always wanted to live in an old house, do it up, you know?"

"I know," she laughed. "That's what I thought when we bought the barn, but I wouldn't want to do it again."

"It is lovely, though," said James, surprising himself. "Worth waiting for."

His mother looked at him and smiled. "Those girls will be waiting if I don't get a move on. They're planning to do a pizza lunch for us all. Maybe you could be setting the table? Now, where are my car keys?"

"In the car, where you left them," said James. "And don't forget to shut the boot!"

Mum left in her usual flurry and the two boys cleared the table. After they'd washed the glasses and jug, they remembered their plan to test the kittens on the equipment.

"I'll set it up, you get the first victim – er … candidate," said Ben. "We'll time him on my stopwatch."

The kittens, refreshed by their nap, were

eager to play and the boys were able to observe each individual quite closely now. This time James made the notes while Ben logged the time taken by the victim (or candidate) to complete the course. If indeed they ever did complete it! Each of the Twins took only half a minute to scratch vaguely at the post before snuggling up to it and falling asleep. The two tabbies were more persistent, sharpening their claws on the upright post, investigating all of the dangling bits, and eventually clambering right up on to the platform.

"Best so far," announced James. "Four different moves in three minutes. They're persistent, those tabbies."

"Even so, I'll bet Big Ginge wins," said Ben. "Go on, bring him out."

James took the second tabby back to the utility room and looked around for Big Ginge. Usually he was easy to find, being so big and so brightly coloured.

But not this time. James looked into the cupboard – a most unlikely place, as the ginger tom rarely joined the others nowadays, preferring to sleep alone on the nearest pile of washing he could find.

"Hurry up! The girls will be back soon and we haven't even started setting the table," Ben called from the kitchen.

"I can't find him," James called back. "Come and help."

So Ben joined him and they both looked round. They checked the washing-machine, the drier, the sink, all the worktops and the laundry baskets (both of them) and still no Ginger.

"Did he go to sleep as soon as you brought him in?" James asked Ben.

Ben stared at him. "I didn't bring him in – you did," he said.

"No, I didn't," said James. "I thought you must have."

"No, you said to bring the sleepy ones in and you'd round up the rest. Ginge was bound to be with the rest."

"No, he wasn't," said James slowly. "I remember thinking it was odd, him joining the sleepy ones. Then Mum called us, and then—"

"Then we forgot to count them all in," concluded Ben.

The two boys stared at each other.

"So he's still out there," said James, swallowing hard. "We've lost him."

"No, we haven't." Ben grabbed his hand. "Come on. He's out there somewhere – we'll find him!"

"And don't forget to shut the door," said James, automatically.

The hunt was on. They started on the terrace, hoping that Ginge wouldn't have found a way off.

"Ginger!" called James. "Come on, kitty, kitty, kitty!" The trouble was, he thought, Ginge didn't know his name. If only Dad had let them give the kittens real names they might have learned to answer to them by now.

"Puss! Puss! Puss! Puss!" hissed Ben, crawling on all fours around the bushes.

"It's no use," said James, almost tearfully. "If he were here he'd have come to play with us by now. He's always the first for a game."

They were at the edge of the terrace now, looking down over the old wall, down the two-metre drop. They stood silently, listening hard, both knowing what they were listening for – the moans of an injured kitten. But all they heard was the clattering of the stream and the sad, solitary cry of a distant curlew, winging over the moor. James thought he'd never felt so alone in his life. He sniffed hard and brushed a hand across his face.

"Come on," said Ben, quietly, gripping his arm. "We'd better go down there and start looking."

Just as they set off, the car pulled into the yard and the girls spilled out. Ben paused for a moment but James wasted no time – he fled down the stone steps into the field. He simply couldn't face them all just then. He felt so stupid – he, of all people, who'd spent so much time with the kittens that Jenny teased him about being a "fussy mother" to them. And now he'd lost one! Oh, if only he'd counted the kittens in, realized Ginger was missing and caught him straight away before he went wandering off on his own! Now they'd all blame him just as he blamed himself. He looked hopelessly down the meadow towards the stream, vaguely conscious of the girls' voices drifting out above him.

"James! James!" The girls weren't calling Ginger, they were calling him back. He looked up to the terrace and saw Ben, gesticulating, beckoning him home. His heart quickened. Could they have found Big Ginge? He ran up the terrace steps, two at a time, and landed, quite out of breath, on the patio.

There he found Mum, smiling broadly, and the girls laughing aloud, holding on to one another and giggling wildly.

"Have you got him?" puffed James. "Where is he?"

Only Ben looked serious. "He's left home, James," he said solemnly. "I'm afraid he did a runner."

"What? Where? How?" James spluttered, catching hold of the edge of the wooden table for support.

Mum put an arm around him. "No need to worry, James," she said. "He's alive and well and living at the stables."

"Living?" James repeated numbly. So it looked as though he'd lost Big Ginge after all. "How did he get there?"

"Sit down and I'll tell you," said Mum, "while Jenny gets us all a drink."

So they all sat round the old wooden table, sipping another jug of juice, while Mum told the story of Big Ginge the Stowaway Kitten.

"Well, I heard some odd squeaks and scratches as I drove down to the stables," she said. "I thought it was only the old car protesting at all the extra work it's been doing lately, but when I pulled in and switched off the engine, the noises didn't stop – in fact, I could hear them coming more clearly, more persistently. So I got out and opened up the boot to check—"

"And out pounced Big Ginger!" laughed Jenny. "He'd been stowing away!"

"Do you know, he stalked across the stable yard as if he'd lived there all his short life, and took up residence in Sheila's office! She runs the stables." Mum finished her story and smiled across at James.

"It was love at first sight!" sighed Rosie, dramatically. "Sheila absolutely fell for him, especially when he leapt up on her desk and killed her pens!"

"You mean she's keeping him?" James asked.

Mum smiled. "Well, for the weekend, on trial," she said gently. "If he settles in all right, he stays. Sheila needs a young cat now her two are getting too old to hunt around the stables."

"Oh, yes, Big Ginger will love it there, won't he, James?" Ben spoke enthusiastically. "He's going to be a great hunter."

James said nothing.

"Funny you should say that," Jenny chimed in. "Sheila said something about calling him a hunter's name. What was it, Rosie?"

"Nimrod, the mighty hunter," Rosie smiled. "We play a piece of music called that, in the school band."

"Who was he?" asked James, interested in spite of himself.

"From the Bible, I think," said Mum. "A famous hunter. Just the name for that kitten and, you must admit, a great improvement on Big Ginge."

Everybody laughingly agreed, except for James, who felt a pang of sadness. Big Ginge had been the biggest, boldest, and, often, the funniest of all the kittens and now he was going to be Nimrod, the mighty mouse-hunter of the stables – not the same adventurous little creature at all.

And, after all, he was the first to leave home.

Chapter 11

Big Ginge did settle happily at the stables. The girls reported seeing him stalking butterflies in Sheila's garden.

"And he likes his new name," said Jenny.

"Nimrod," James muttered into his cornflakes. "What a name for a cat!"

"It's a good name for *that* cat," said Jenny. "Don't you think it suits him?"

But nothing suited James that Saturday morning. It wasn't only the loss of a kitten that left him feeling so gloomy. Ben's parents had already arrived – the holiday was over. From now on it was all farewells: first Nimrod, then Ben, and, gradually, the rest of the kittens would be going until there'd be only himself and Breakfast left to comfort one another.

Not that Breakfast needed any comforting – she was sprightly as a kitten herself now that her offspring were fully weaned – well, almost all: the Tiny Twins sidled up to her now and then for a little comforting snack.

"It's just a habit," Dad assured James, when he pointed out they weren't ready to leave their mother. "They'll forget all about mother's milk once they're at Carol's."

James put down his spoon and sighed deeply. Of all the kittens in the entire litter, he thought, those Twins were the least suited to be going out into the world. He did want them to stay together and the mill seemed to be the only place that wanted two cats. But they seemed so frail, so small... James found himself near to tears just thinking about them.

It was only the sound of the phone that stopped the tearful flow. James sniffed hard and picked up the receiver.

"Hi! James?" It was Ben.

"Yes," said James, cautiously. No use

getting excited about a call from Ben – he was
due to go back to London any minute. "You
still here?"

"Yes, and guess what?"

"What?" Again James wouldn't let himself
get excited. They wouldn't have agreed to
leave Ben up here, would they?

"We're renting a cottage up here for the
summer – a base for house-hunting."

"Oh, good."

"So, you see, I'll be living close by, and going to your school eventually and—"

"And when?"

"Well, Dad's coming up to his new job next month but Mum says I've got to finish this term at my old school – you know, exams and all that. But we'll be up here in time for the summer holidays."

"Oh, great!" James tried to sound enthusiastic but the summer holidays seemed years away just then.

"But here's the really good news," Ben went on, then paused, waiting for James's reaction. He wasn't disappointed.

"Go on!" urged James, roused at last.

"They've said I can have one of your kittens – if you can keep it until we move north, that is."

"Of course we can," said James, recklessly. "Which one?"

"Can we come round to see them?"

"Yes. When?"

"Right now," said Ben. "We've got a lot to do today. See you!"

"See yah!" said James, as they did at school, then he ran upstairs to break the news to his sleeping parents that they had visitors arriving any minute.

Rosie came too, so that there was almost a party spirit around the kitchen table as James and Jenny brought coffee. The parents talked houses, Rosie and Jenny talked horses, and Ben and James went to collect the kittens.

They came bounding across to the boys as soon as the door was opened – all except for the Twins, who were snuggled up to Breakfast in the old box.

"They need a few more weeks with their mother. They're nowhere near ready to leave," James said sadly.

"Well, why don't you leave them here? We can take one and somebody else could have the other."

James shook his head. "I think they should stay together. That's why I thought the mill would be the best place. But they haven't grown up as fast as the others, and I know

Dad can't wait to move them in, and..." His voice faltered.

Embarrassed, Ben turned away to watch the two tabbies pacing up and down in front of the end window, watching out for anything that moved.

"Hey, I've got an idea!" he said suddenly.

"Have you?" James sniffed hard. "What about?"

"That pair over there – and the Tiny Twins, too. Remember our test? The Twins were useless, far too babyish to take them seriously, but the tabbies were brilliant."

"Yes, I remember they came out top because we'd just lost Big Ginger." James turned to look at the pair of kittens, who ignored everything except the window. He smiled for the very first time that morning. "If only we can persuade Dad."

"Maybe we can!" Ben produced the battered little pad from the back pocket of his jeans. "I'm going to put the results on my computer and send you a print-out, but these rough notes will have to do for now."

"They'll do," said James, decisively. "Come on, let's talk to Dad."

The kittens spilled out into the kitchen with them; even the Twins put in an appearance, and Breakfast presided over them all as if showing them off.

"I love that little black and white one there," Ben's mother said, nodding over to one of the Tiny Twins. "So beautifully marked."

"This one, you mean?" asked her husband, picking up Twin B.

"No, that one over there close to its mother."

"Well, this one's got nice markings, too."

"No, the other one's better." She leaned over and picked up Twin A.

Mr Bowers looked from one kitten to the other. "They both look the same to me," he said.

"They are," laughed Jenny. "Identical. James says they're twins."

"Twins? How sweet!" Mrs Bowers gently stroked the kitten's nose. "Imagine – identical twins!"

"Now then, Karen, don't get carried away," warned her husband.

"Of course not," she said. "I'm not suggesting we take two." But there was a wistful note in her voice. Ben looked at James and winked.

But James's dad shook his head. "Those two are spoken for anyway," he said. "They're off to my workshop next week-end."

James looked up, startled. He hadn't expected it to be so soon.

"Oh, but they're so tiny," murmured Mrs Bowers.

"They'll soon grow," smiled Dad.

"Go on!" Ben nudged James hard and thrust the notebook into his hand. "Now!"

"Well, actually, Dad," said James, hesitantly, "I don't think they're going to be much use over at the mill..."

"Oh, come on, James! You've always been soppy about those twins," said Jenny.

"No, this isn't soppy, this is, er..." He looked at Ben for support.

"Scientific," said Ben firmly.

The girls snorted but Ben merely ignored them.

"We did some tests," he said, determinedly, "and they proved that the Twins aren't exactly the brightest of the bunch. Go on, James, show them the results."

So James opened up the notebook and showed Dad the notes he'd made – was it only yesterday morning?

"Ben's going to put them through his computer," he said breathlessly "and send us a print-out, but you can see who the winners were – look!"

"Timing, concentration, completing the course – they came top in everything." Ben pointed at the scribbled figures.

His father laughed. "Trust you to find some work to do when you're supposed to be on holiday," he said.

But James's dad was reading the notebook and nodding, thoughtfully. "This is an excellent piece of observation," he said. "Well done, Ben."

"It was James who invented the apparatus," said Ben. "I only timed the tests."

"And I thought that equipment was for the kittens to play on," Jenny said, indignantly. "Just for fun."

"It was fun," smiled Ben, "for the kittens."

"For you two, more like." Jenny glowered at him.

"I expect the kittens enjoyed all the attention they got," said her mother, soothingly.

"Yes, just like the obstacle course in the paddock," Rosie pointed out. "It's really for training but the ponies love doing it."

"Well, I'm impressed," said James's dad. He handed the notebook back to Ben and turned to smile at James. "I think the tabbies will be better down at the mill than your Tiny Twins."

"Thanks, Dad." James grinned so broadly his face almost split in two.

"So we can have one of the black-and-whites, can we?" asked Mrs Bowers. "Go on, Ben, you choose. Though how you can tell the difference I don't know."

James was about to interrupt but Ben nudged him – with the edge of his notebook this time. Then there was a pause while Ben flicked through the pages.

"Our observations show that the two black-and-white kittens really do behave like twins. They do everything together – eat, drink, sleep, play – and whenever we separated them they just curled up or sat pining for the other one."

He looked across at his dad and smiled, sweetly. "Interesting, wasn't it?"

Mr Bowers smiled back. "All right, budding scientist, you've convinced me." He turned to his wife. "I suppose we'll just have to take both, if only to keep Ben's notebook up to date."

Everyone was smiling now, cuddling kittens, laughing and talking. James and Ben said nothing, merely grinned at each other.

"Well, if we're going to give a home to two kittens, we'd better find one for ourselves." Ben's father stood up. "Come on, Ben, time to go."

It wasn't so hard saying goodbye to Ben now that James really did know he'd be coming back, and now that the Tiny Twins were reprieved. While everyone else was out in the yard saying farewells, James took the kittens back to the utility room. The Tiny Twins, as usual, snuggled in their box; the tabbies, as usual, went to gaze hopefully out of the window, waiting to catch a passing bird. Suddenly, James felt something pressing on the toe of his sneaker – it was the smoky-grey kitten, the quiet one, scarcely ever noticed in all the hurly-burly of feline life. James looked down at her and she raised her blue-green eyes up to him, purring softly.

"Hey, Smoky!" James bent to pick her up. "You've never had much attention, have you – what with big, bold Nimrod and the other two couples? You've been left out of things rather." The kitten snuggled under his neck and tickled his chin. "I know how you feel," said James, only half-laughing. "And now you're the only one without a home to go to." He paused at the door. "Unless..." he said to himself. He put her down gently and closed the door.

The following weekend they took the tabbies over to Carol's. She didn't mind having tabbies instead of black-and-whites.

"They'll match the stone and wood dust that hangs around here," she pointed out. "And just look at them settling in!"

The tabbies, released from the travelling basket, had prowled around the flat until they discovered the narrow windows with deep sills in the end gable. Now they were sitting, one to each window, gazing ecstatically up into the sky.

"They're bird-watchers," James explained.

"I hope they're mouse-watchers as well," said Carol.

"Oh, they're going to be good hunters. James tested them and he's got the results to prove it," said Dad. "Show her Ben's chart."

So James opened up the much-fingered chart that Ben had sent him and showed Carol how the tabbies had performed in their tests.

"You see, Big Ginge – I mean Nimrod – was also the clumsiest. Kept knocking the apparatus over. Then the Tiny Twins – well, they hadn't a clue. Never even got started. But the tabbies were quick, neat and seemed to know just what they were doing. *And* they got the cheese at the top."

"What's this one?" Carol pointed to the fourth name on the chart.

"Oh, that's the grey one," said Jenny. "She's so beautiful now – her coat's smooth and sleek but really thick, and her eyes are a brilliant blue."

"Green," said James, at the same time. They both laughed. This argument had been running all week.

"But what's this query about her results?" asked Carol.

"Ah, well, you see..." James took a deep breath. He'd been looking for the right opportunity to bring this up with his parents, and this looked like it. "Smoky-grey didn't climb on the apparatus at first, she just prowled round, sort of sizing it up. We thought she was going to lose time like that. But when she did move – well, she shot up the pole, ignored all the obstacles and went straight on to the cheese in the cage. Fastest time, but never did the tests."

"Clever cat," Carol laughed. "Straight for the food!"

"Like her mother," said Mum. "Remember, James, how she came to eat your breakfast when we first moved in?"

James nodded. "Smoky-grey *is* like Breakfast," he said. "Haven't you seen them sitting on the terrace wall together?" He took a deep breath. "So I was wondering ... I mean, as we haven't found a home for her..."

"Yet," said Mum.

"Well, you see..."

"Why don't we keep her?" finished Jenny, reading his mind. "She'll be company for Breakfast when we're out all day. They get on so well."

Mum looked at Dad. "What do you think?" she asked.

Dad shrugged. "Well, we've found homes for five of them," he said. "Five out of six – not bad."

"And one out of six can stay?" asked Jenny.

"Anything to stop you nagging for a pony," grinned Dad.

"Oh, I don't need a pony now we're so close to the stables," said Jenny, happily.

"And I wouldn't want a dog now we've got two cats," said James.

"Four actually," Mum reminded him. "It'll be some weeks yet before the Bowers send for the Twins."

"Well, I don't envy you," said Carol. "I've an idea I'm going to have my hands full with these two."

They left the tabbies, still keeping watch

up into the skies, quite oblivious of the family's departure.

"They didn't even look up to say goodbye," Jenny complained on the way home.

"That shows they're happy," said James.

And so was he. He had no worries about the Tiny Twins now. They were getting less tiny and more twinny every day. He had a new best friend who would soon be coming up to live close by, and a new kitten as well as his beautiful Breakfast. Yes, he was very happy now.

On Monday morning everyone was dashing around as usual, showering, dressing, grabbing a coffee, a bit of toast. Only James sat at the kitchen table, slurping cornflakes and reading Ben's chart for the umpteenth time. Until he heard a small squeak, a tiny miaow. He looked down and there was Smoky-grey, all on her own, sitting at the foot of his stool and gazing up at him with her blue-green eyes.

"Hello, Smoky," he said, picking up a cat bowl. "Have you come to finish my breakfast?"

HIPPO ANIMAL

Have you ever longed for a puppy to love, or a horse of your own? Have you ever wondered what it would be like to make friends with a wild animal? If so, then you're sure to fall in love with these fantastic titles from Hippo Animal!

Owl Cry
Deborah van der Beek
Can Solomon really look after an abandoned baby owl?

Thunderfoot
Deborah van der Beek
When Mel finds the enormous, neglected horse Thunderfoot, she doesn't know it will change her life for ever...

Vanilla Fudge
Deborah van der Beek
When Lizzie and Hannah fall in love with the same dog, neither of them will give up without a fight...

A Foxcub Named Freedom
Brenda Jobling
An injured vixen nudges her young son away from her. She can sense danger and cares nothing for herself – only for her son's freedom...

Goose on the Run
Brenda Jobling

It's an unusual pet – an injured Canada goose.
But soon Josh can't imagine being without him.
And the goose won't let *anyone* take him away
from Josh...

Pirate the Seal
Brenda Jobling

Ryan's always been lonely – but then he meets
Pirate and at last he has a real friend...

Animal Rescue
Bette Paul

Can Tessa help save the badgers of Delves Wood
from destruction?

Take Six Kittens
Bette Paul

James and Jenny's dad promises them a pet when
they move to the country. But they end up with
more than they bargained for...

Take Six Puppies
Bette Paul

Anna knows she shouldn't get attached to the
six new puppies at the Millington Farm Dog
Sanctuary, but surely it can't hurt to get just a
little bit fond of them...